The Pı

MW01134649

Cover design copyright © 2017 by Jenni James

Copyright© 2017 by Jenni James

SERENITY BROOKE PRESS

This book is for my dearest Sylvie.
Your prince is coming,
I promise.

CHAPTER ONE:

Princess Kyra Marie's heart pounded as she gripped the sides of Thunder and held on tight. The horse's hooves crushed the muddy path as the torrential storm raged around them. How grateful she was for that storm! It was probably the only thing keeping her safe from the bandits that had frightened her horses and capsized the carriage she had been riding in.

"Run, Thunder, run!" she shouted over the hooves and the rain. She was not certain the horse could hear her. "Go!"

A large bang and then another could be heard far behind. She dug her heels into the horse and clung on as tight as she could, her face buried into Thunder's neck and flinging mane. What she wouldn't give for her sidesaddle at this moment! Or even her father's gentleman's saddle. Either would be preferred to this bare-backed bouncing she was experiencing and the slipperiness of the horse below.

And yet, by some small miracle, they raced on. She did not want to think of the loud banging she had heard. It sounded most definitely like gunshots, and her poor coachman, footman, outriders, and maid were still back there. "Run!"

Moments before in the muddle of the coach overturning, she had felt rough arms drag her from the carriage and swing her onto the horse. Jasper's eyes as he met hers were frightened, but determined. "Ride to safety, Your Highness. Go now!" the coachman had shouted.

"You are injured!" she gasped, her frantic gaze taking in the blood on his brow and arm. "I cannot leave you in this state."

"I am fine! It is you they are after! Find the nearest shelter and send word to your father. Go, Princess! They are coming!" He had slapped the horse's rear with the reins he had removed, causing it to bolt. It was all Kyra could do to hold on as Thunder leaped forward and began to gallop.

"Did the bandits shoot Jasper? Did they shoot everyone?" She did not know. She did not dare go back to see. Onward Thunder struck the muddy ground, and forward she flew.

It was several more minutes—or perhaps an hour, she was not certain—but eventually, her horse became tired and was heaving greatly. Her heart clenched in fear. Though she had not heard anyone pursuing them, it was still terrifying. The darkness was closing in, and the rain continued to beat down severely. She slowly brought Thunder to a walk and attempted to peer through the torrent to the wilderness before them.

Where could she be? Kyra had been traveling to the sea, to another kingdom, to meet a prince who had hoped to form an alliance with her family. It was all a political move put together by her parents. Her mother assured her that if they did not suit, she was not bound to wed him. All of that was grand, but she was supposed to be there in two days, and it did not seem possible. Meanwhile, it would appear that she was in a neighboring kingdom somewhere in the middle, on a muddied path her horse had chosen to follow off the main road and between what looked to be crop fields.

Kyra sighed and pulled Thunder to a stop, leading him to a small puddle of water amidst the crops to allow him some sort of relief. He lapped for a bit while she walked onward and attempted to place where they were. Honestly, she had been a dreadful student during her land study courses, and knew next to nothing of any kingdom but hers. She did not believe she would need to know about the geography of anyone else's land but her family's. The clouds could be hiding several mountains, but from what she could see, it was severely flat all around. Just fields and fields of farmland—not even a cottage to shed light. One would think that with all the produce, there would be several cottages.

She wiped the wetness from her eyes and turned around. "Goodness!" she gasped. "Well, there may be help after all."

Somehow they had managed to pass by a large fortress-type castle not a quarter of a mile behind them. Surrounding the castle was the village. She shook her head and marveled at the level of foolishness to miss something so large. Who knows how long she would have wandered without seeing it. "Come, Thunder," she said as she lifted her soaking, filthy skirts and walked over to the large white horse. "I do not know about you, but I could use some respite. Let us pray that this kingdom is friendly."

She attempted to get back on the horse several times, but came slipping down over and over again. "Oh, for goodness' sake!" Finally, Kyra gave up, and gently tugging upon Thunder's mane, she began to walk through the ankle-deep sludge toward the castle ahead. By the time she got there, the rest of her hair had completely fallen from its pins, and she no doubt looked more a muddy wraith than a royal princess.

The castle guards came forward and met her upon the bridge above the moat. "What business do you have here, miss?" asked an older man with kindly eyes.

Kyra was just about to announce her name and the kingdom she was from when several riders came past, one bringing in Lightning, the matching gelding to Thunder, and her heart dropped. The two horses neighed in acknowledgement as they passed each other. Were these the bandits who were after her? What else had they stolen? Where was everyone else? Did they truly shoot them? Her stomach felt ill. She should not have come here. Of all the places to seek refuge.

"Miss? Are you all right?"

Mercifully, none of the men who passed seemed to recognize her or Thunder. She probably had the weather and poor visibility to thank for that.

"Miss?"

Suddenly, she glanced up at the man before her. "Forgive me. I am lost and became detached from my traveling party. I came here to seek shelter, but perhaps this place is too fancy for me. I will seek elsewhere."

"No, I have orders that all foreigners must come up to the castle." When she hesitated, he continued, "They are kind—you will be safe. And perhaps they can help locate your party."

"What about my horse?" she asked, attempting to buy some time.

"We will keep him in the stables until you are allowed to leave."

"Allowed to leave?" Her eyebrows rose. Why did it seem as though she would be held as a prisoner? The man began to walk toward the large fortress. Nervously, Kyra looked around her, but with the other guards staring, she did not dare run away. Instead, she pushed her fears aside, gathered her skirts, and followed him over the slick cobblestone. One thing was for certain—she would tell them her name was Marie. If they were the ones who had overturned her coach, she would have to tread very cautiously indeed.

Before they made it to the main structure, a man came with a rope and took Thunder away. It was not until that moment that she felt officially alone.

As the guard stepped through a lighted corridor and into the rich expanse of building, Kyra swallowed the lump in her throat and pressed forward. They wound through several passages and up a flight of stairs before the guard stopped in front of intricately chiseled wooden doors and rapped upon them swiftly with a cane. The doors silently opened to reveal a large room with two empty thrones in the center.

"Stay here," the guard told her as she walked in. "Someone will be with you shortly." And then he left. Just like that. A small boy in elaborate clothes shut the door behind the guard as he walked out and then stood in front of it with his arms folded, as if blocking her way.

Did they honestly believe he was adequate security? He could not have been more than six or seven years old. She smothered a grin and then turned back toward the large thrones before her. And waited, wishing more than anything that she was not quite so filthy.

About ten minutes later, a tall, finely dressed young man came into the room from a side door and then glanced around before addressing her. "Has no one been here to help you?"

"I—uh, no." Kyra held her hands together in front of her so they would not tremble.

"Forgive us. We are not usually so discourteous to guests."

She smiled nervously. His light brown hair matched his skin tone perfectly, and his voice was a bit deeper than any young man she had ever heard speak before. Goodness, he was handsome. "Who are you?"

He grinned and bowed low. "I am Prince David of the Haltaen Court, at your service. Now may I be so bold as to ask whom I am speaking with?"

"Oh!" She curtsied before him, her ragged skirts smearing the pristine floor as she did so. Her gaze met his, and she froze. His green eyes were positively hypnotizing. "I am Prince—" She gasped and coughed. "Excuse me. I am Marie. I was traveling with a party and got lost in the storm, so I have come here to ask for refuge. Yet, as you can see, I am a little more shabbily dressed than I would prefer to be at this time. I understand completely if you would wish me away immediately. I will go and seek shelter elsewhere."

"Marie?" He walked over to her with a quizzical look upon his face. "Is that what you are called?"

Her heart began to race again. "Yes, Your Highness."

"No surname?"

"Well, no."

He stepped even closer to her. Indeed, they were less than half a meter away. "And where did you say you were from?"

"I did not."

He waited with a handsome brow lifted, and so she finally answered the truth. "I am from Dillany, Your Highness."

"Dillany! That is a very beautiful place."

"Thank you. I believe so as well."

Prince David took a few steps back and then continued, "So tell me, Miss Marie, do all people of Dillany speak so perfectly as you do, or just the royalty?"

Kyra's jaw dropped. She did not know how to answer him. Just then, an older woman came bursting into the room.

"David! I see you are with the visitor. I am so sorry, my dear. We have been extremely busy with a last-minute discussion. I did not mean to keep you waiting."

This must be the queen. Kyra curtsied again. "Your Majesty."

"My guard has said you have lost your way, and you were with a traveling party. Did this party perchance have an exceptionally pretty white horse to match your own?"

She swallowed and willed her voice to answer evenly. "I—uh, I do not believe so."

CHAPTER TWO:

After they sent the girl away with a maid to be cleaned up, Queen Genevieve turned to her son. "She is telling us a falsehood. I cannot for one minute imagine she is truly a mere commoner, yet why would she lie? Why pretend as if she were below her station?"

"She may talk like us, Mother, but how do you really know she is not telling the truth?"

"Her dress!" The queen walked over to her throne and sat upon it. "Trust me, David, if you understood fashion as I do, you would have noted the fabric of her gown. You cannot tell me a simple commoner could afford such material, filthy or not. No. It is all a ruse to confuse us."

"Do you believe she is royalty, then?"

She tapped her fingers upon the arm of her throne. "I do not know what to believe. However, I am certain she is not what she seems." She glanced over at him suddenly. "And the horses! You do not know. You were not in that meeting. The horse she was with—which strangely had no saddle whatsoever—matches the gelding the guards found at the borders of our kingdom. Any fool can see the two horses know each other. I went and saw for myself. They were whinnying back and forth in the stables like long-lost friends. There is something very suspicious going on here, and until we get to the bottom of it, I want you to be cautious around the girl."

"Do you think she is a threat to the kingdom?"

His mother shook her head. "How should I know? Our men said that shots were fired, a carriage overturned, and a horse found. Nothing else worth note was left in the carriage—though it was a very fine one indeed. And now this girl shows up to the castle, lying about who she is. She knows something here, and is refusing to speak the truth. It is definitely not all as it seems."

"What are we to do, then?" David's concern was not for the untidy chit, but much more for his mother's anxious nature. "Truly, if the girl is not what she seems, why not send her out packing? We have no need for this type of nonsense here. Or for anyone's lies."

"Your father will decide. Until then, we will be kind as always—but keep your distance. Something has happened to a very dignified person in that coach, and we need to know what it was and see if we could help them. Heavens, someone—or several someones—could be kidnapped at this moment. And the girl may have been involved in their disappearance."

David cleared his throat. "Right. Tonight I will begin sending queries out to all the kingdoms with descriptions of the horses, the girl, and the carriage. Maybe we will be able to sort out some clues that way."

The queen continued to tap her fingers on the throne. "What if one of the other kingdoms attacked the carriage? Then they would be aware that we are searching for them. It may harm the passengers even more."

"Then why worry about this at all? Why not leave it for the kingdoms to sort out?"

"Are you jesting, my son? This happened on our land. No one breaks the treaties on our land and we not get to sort it out. No, your father is even now working with the guards to see what can be done. Meanwhile, treat young Miss Marie as you would any visitor, with perhaps more supervision and caution, and mention not a word of any of this to her."

"Very good."

"Oh, and David. If she is royalty, we will know soon enough."

He grinned. Nothing slipped by his mother. "And how is that?"

She chuckled. "We shall do as she wishes and treat her as a commoner. Put her to work, so to speak. Perhaps in the pea fields a few hours a day. If she is a true princess, she will not be able to stand the work, nor will she have any notion of what she is supposed to be doing. I give her three days, tops, amongst the crops of peas, and she will be begging to return home."

"Do you mean to change her bedroom as well? I had her sent to the guest wing."

She waved her hand. "No, of course not. Let the girl at least get some sort of rest. The poor thing was drenched. I do not imply to give her hard menial labor all day long and then put her up in the attics with the servants. Heavens! She would be useless. No, I am only hoping to ferret out her secrets. So in every other aspect, she will be treated as a guest—comfortably. Until we know if she is a villainess, she is to be given certain liberties as we continue to investigate where she came from and just who she really is."

"Are you saying to act as if it is common for all of us to work out in the fields?" David was not quite sure he liked where his mother's thoughts were heading.

"Well, why not? It would not be too awful for us to head out there and see how she does, would it?" She thought for a minute and then said, "You know, I change my mind, son. I think you would be the perfect foil to actually bring the truth out. I know I mentioned a moment ago to stay clear of her, but I believe—and I think your father will agree—that to keep our little kingdom safe, it is best to have you with her as much as possible, and then be sure to report each night what you have found out that day."

"And that means helping with the pea fields as well?"

"Only a little while a day. Nothing drastic. You are at least informed in how to do so. You have had the charge over the produce nearly two months at least."

Yes, but that was from the comfort of his saddle. David sighed. It was absolutely useless to attempt to disagree with the queen when she was in one of her intrigues. It was best to go along with it as she suggested, for he found out years ago that his mother was rarely wrong in her assessments. Therefore, if she believed the kingdom was safer with him tending to the girl, she would most definitely be right. "Very well. I shall begin in the morning." And he wished fervently that the mysterious girl would be gone as soon as possible so his life might return to normal once more.

CHAPTER THREE:

After her glorious bath, where the maid had put fresh lavender and vanilla beans in the water to steam with her, Kyra stepped into a borrowed dressing gown and padded upon thick carpet into the guest chamber. It was a beautiful room decorated in a multicolored floral design. Pinks, blues, yellows, purples, reds—absolutely stunning. There was a small wardrobe, a pretty little secretary to write on, a large chaise lounge near the window, and a very regal bed. Indeed, the top of the mattress came to eye level. Thank goodness there was a small ladder next to the headboard.

Kyra grinned at the opulence this kingdom showed their guests. One never knew what customs another country had until one actually lived them. Curious, she walked over to the bed and lifted the counterpane to see just how they made such a large mattress. She chuckled when she revealed not one mattress, but several stacked upon each other!

What an oddity.

The maid had said she had brought in some older gowns for Kyra to try on and hopefully find a couple that worked. She walked over to the wardrobe and discovered nearly ten gowns awaiting her inspection. Such generosity. Surely a kingdom as generous as this could not be the type that went around attacking coaches. "Though, perhaps the kindness was a ruse to hide away other nefarious secrets," she muttered under her breath.

Kyra shuddered as apprehension began to creep its way into her heart again. The sooner she was away from this place, the better.

Someone knocked upon the door. "Miss Marie," the maid said as Kyra opened it. "Her Majesty inquires if you would enjoy some tea brought to your room. The family has already partaken of supper, but she is more than eager to send up some refreshment, if you would so like."

"Thank you. I am nearly famished." Kyra looked imploringly at the girl. "Tell Her Majesty how grateful I am that she has thought of me, and let her know the gowns will suit just fine." Even if they did not fit, Kyra had no intention of imposing upon them further.

"Very good, miss." The maid bobbed a curtsy and headed out the door. "Tea will be brought up in a moment."

With that, Kyra quickly slipped on a blue frock, one not too elaborate, and yet not too plain, either. She found a comb in the attached dressing room and began to work through her clean hair. It took no time at all to braid it and throw it over her shoulder.

When tea came, it had everything a hungry princess could ask for. Delicious scones, jams, cold meats, cheeses, fruit, and even sweet biscuits and chocolate cake. The rich herbal blend of floral and spices in the tea was surprisingly good as well. Kyra made short work of the meal, eating as though she had not for days. Her mother would be appalled, but since no one was around, who would ever be the wiser?

"Well, I'll be!" exclaimed the maid as she entered a little later. "You clean devoured the tea in record time."

Kyra gave a rueful grin and bit her lip. "I was dreadfully hungry."

"You must have been. I have never seen anyone eat as you do, and I have been working at this castle full on six years now."

Kyra blushed and then decided to change the subject as best she could. "The actual tea was wonderful. Does your cook blend her own?"

"Of course she does!" The maid beamed. "Right proud of her teas we are, too. If you liked that one, you haven't tried nothing yet. Wait until she decides to share the peppermint—that one's my favorite!"

It was refreshing to see such pride amongst the staff toward each other. They must be a tight-knit group. "I would love to try it. And as you take the tray down, please let her know how much I appreciated all of it. Marvelous cook you have. She must be the jewel of the kitchens."

"She is, miss! And I'll be right quick to tell her you said so, too."

Once the maid left, Kyra wandered over to the window and looked out into the storm that was still rampant. At once, she was reminded of all those who had been traveling with her. What was their state? Were their stomachs full? Did they have somewhere warm to sleep? And then the question that burned most within her—were they even still alive?

She sat down upon the chaise lounge and questioned all that was raging around her. Though she felt safe, she wished her mother or father were here—someone to guide her in what to do. All her life, she had been sheltered and indulged. Now that she was away from home on her first real adventure and everything had gone wrong, she realized just how alone she really was. It was as if she was trapped here until she could find a way out again. "Though who knows how long that may be," she muttered. Her heart clenched as waves of sadness and fear pummeled it. How she wished it were all a dream.

Yet it was not! People—dear people she loved and cared for—were in danger, and she had no way of knowing what to do.

That night after she climbed up the ladder to get into bed, she lay awake reliving the startling crash over and over again. In doing so, she began to recollect each painful bruise on her body from the ordeal. Yet she fretted most for those loved ones she could not see. The coachman, her maid, the outriders. How had they fared?

For hours, her mind reeled and raced over questions she could not answer as she tossed and turned upon the odd bed. Each time she would flip from one side to the other, it felt as if the whole lot of mattresses would tumble off. Indeed, it was an extremely awkward setup, and she wondered if any guest got a wink of sleep in this castle. The silly tower of mattresses was definitely not as comfortable as one would think.

By the morning, Kyra had become more exhausted than rested, and had definite cause to wonder if she managed to get any sleep at all.

CHAPTER FOUR:

"Good morning!" declared the queen as Kyra, dressed in a fine yellow gown, followed the maid into the breakfast room. The queen wore a long dark-purple gown and stood next to a buffet table laden full with all sorts of covered silver dishes. It reminded Kyra a bit of the breakfast room at home.

"Thank you, Your Majesty." Kyra curtsied. "And a good morning to you, as well."

The queen smiled and then asked, "And how did you sleep?"

Kyra nodded as brightly as possible and politely lied. "Wonderfully. Your guest room is very inviting. Thank you for all you have done to guarantee that I am well provided for. You are too kind."

"Nonsense." The older woman brushed away her words. "Now, tell me, before my son and husband join us, how do the gowns fit? This one looks a little big, but you wear it well. Are the others adequate, or do you need me to send for more clothes?"

Goodness. "No, do not trouble yourself. I have more than enough to choose from in the wardrobe, I am sure. Though to be honest, I have not tried them all on as of yet."

"Of course not. You were probably too exhausted from your travels and wanderings to concentrate on anything but sleep."

Kyra glanced away. Before she could answer, Prince David and the king came walking in together.

"Well, you must be our visitor!" the king boomed as he strode over and clasped her hand.

"I . . . yes, Your Majesty." She dipped a low curtsy and allowed the older man to pull her up.

"And how do you fare? Are you well? I hear you were separated from your party. Dreadful shame!" He glanced up at his wife and then smiled back at Kyra. "You are more than welcome to use anything you need to write letters and the like. Do not hesitate to ask should you require something. I am sure you are eager to contact your family."

Yes. She must contact them. "Thank you, Your Majesty. I am very keen to do so."

He nodded. "Yes, I assumed so. I can imagine they will be most worried about you." He collected a plate from the table and began to fill it up. "Was it your family you were traveling with?"

"I—" She caught the eye of Prince David and quickly looked away. "I was not traveling with family."

The king paused with his fork over a large platter of ham. "Really? Then who were you traveling with, might I ask?"

He would know in a heartbeat the carriage was hers. "A few personal friends. I was on my way to meet my betrothed."

"Truly?" The queen held a plate in her hand and stared at Kyra. "You are betrothed? I was not aware you were of marrying age. Indeed, you look quite young."

Many people had told her she appeared younger than the seventeen she was. "Yes and no." Kyra purposely did not look at the prince again. "I was told to meet him first and see how we suited before making my decision."

"Your decision?" The king laughed. "Must be nice to have parents who care what your thoughts are! Many of us are put into positions where we are not given that liberty."

"Yes, my parents are very forward thinkers."

She heard a distinct chuckle from the prince, but she did not dare look over. Was he mocking her?

The queen collected some boiled eggs from a silver bowl and then handed Kyra the spoon. "Please eat as much as you would like. I hear you have quite the appetite for one so small."

Kyra blushed, quickly took the spoon from her, and blindly filled her plate with a little of everything on the table.

"Come, Miss Marie. You may sit with David while we eat." The queen pointed to two empty chairs near them.

Did they always make it a habit to eat with their visitors, no matter their social status? Indeed, they must be the most generous king and queen—or the most superficial, where they pretended to host commoners. For her part, Kyra was inclined to believe they were sadly insincere. Nothing they had done upon her arrival, after the initial bath, had helped her feel more at ease. In fact, she was becoming more and more unsettled by the moment. She took a deep breath and said simply, "Thank you again for your hospitality. I will write to my family as you suggest, and then I will most likely head out this afternoon. I am very concerned my party will be searching for me, and I hope nothing has happened to them."

"You cannot go out in this state!" the queen insisted. "You do not know where you are, or where your traveling partners could be. Anything could happen to you on those roads. No, I insist you stay here until we can locate your parents. Please have a seat and join us."

Were they to hold her prisoner, then? A small fissure of fear went up her spine as she sat down next to the handsome prince. This ruse was becoming too overwhelming for her. How much longer must she pretend to be someone she was not? And what was to become of her if they found out the truth? Slowly, she chewed upon the meat and fruit on her plate, forcing each mouthful down as the king and queen continued to dominate the conversation.

"David is to go out into the fields this afternoon, and we thought it would be an enjoyable experience for you to help out and get to know the ways of our land."

Kyra was not sure if she wanted to be anywhere with the prince. And she had no notion of what the queen referred to when she mentioned they were to go out into the fields. Were they to walk out in them for exercise, then? She took another bite of food and then noticed that all three sets of eyes were staring at her, waiting for a response. She swallowed and then attempted a smile. "Thank you. It sounds lovely."

"It will certainly be interesting." She caught the prince's gaze and was amazed to see a smirk about his features.

Was he mocking her again? Kyra sat up more primly in her chair and raised her nose a notch. "I noticed your fields last night. What do you grow in them?"

"Peas." The queen let out a small chuckle. She too seemed to give off an air of disbelief, or mockery, or something.

It felt as though Kyra had been placed in the middle of a jest of some sort, and it was completely disconcerting. Not one to allow tomfoolery to best her, she asked simply, "Is there something amiss? Something here I am not aware of?"

The king smiled a genuine smile and said, "Miss Marie, there is nothing you should fear. This outing David is to take you on is something every commoner should easily be able to accomplish. It will get you outside, enjoying a bit of fresh air, and allow you to see how our kingdom works until we can hear back from your family."

The king and queen exchanged a look. "Yes, dear. In exchange for our hospitality, we allow you a chance to go out into the fields."

What in heaven's name was going on? It was as if she had stepped into the pages of a melodramatic novel. Though, on second thought, the queen's calm smile looked genuine. Kyra took a deep breath. If she was not careful, she would become suspicious of absolutely everything, and the last thing she needed was to show them how fidgety she had become. Especially if this particular royal family turned out to be her enemy. "It sounds delightful."

CHAPTER FIVE:

David turned from the window in the west drawing room and answered his mother. "We will be back in time for high tea. Please see that we have some sandwiches, as I am certain to be rather famished. More famished than I have ever been before."

"Oh, bosh!" The queen fluttered her hand. "Do not be so dramatic, son. Perhaps I should have you work in the fields more often, if this is to be your response. Our people tend the peas just fine, and they have never complained of the long hours."

"To you," he said archly.

She huffed and picked up her embroidery just as Miss Marie's steps could be heard on the stairs. "She is coming. Try to find out who she really is. Charm her, if you must," the queen hissed.

Miss Marie came into the room and curtsied to them both.

"Welcome!" His mother waved her in. "And how does the bonnet suit?" she asked the girl.

David looked on as Marie smiled and placed the yellow hat upon her head. "Thank you. It is very pretty, Your Majesty, and seems to fit perfectly."

"Splendid." The queen glanced at David. "Enjoy yourselves. Today should prove to be very interesting."

"Interesting" was not the word he would have chosen for it. David stifled a sigh and held out his arm as he sauntered over to her. "Shall we proceed, Miss Marie?" he asked with as much dignity as possible.

"Certainly, Your Highness." She slipped her hand into the crook of his elbow and walked with him out the door, down the hallway, through the entrance of the castle, and into the waiting carriage.

David had one thought and one thought only—to get through this day and this awful errand as quickly as possible. And he had every intention of doing just that until—

"I cannot believe this is the same palace I found last night. Why, it is positively enchanting!" Miss Marie was bent over awkwardly, gazing out of the carriage window in such a way, she could see upwards as well as directly in front. "I have never seen its equal. Truly your family must be exceptionally proud to own such a place."

"I . . . uh, I have never thought of it." Strange how such an excited comment could make him pause. He moved over and attempted the same pose as she, curious as to what had captured her so. Indeed, the castle looked triumphant and shimmered beautifully with its white stone walls, blue slate turrets, and stained-glass windows.

Suddenly, she leaned back into the seat of the carriage as it began to pull forward and nearly hit him. "Oh, I am so sorry. Forgive me, Your Highness. I did not know you were so close."

David felt his cheeks growing warm. "How would you have known? I gave you no warning at all. Forgive me. The fault is all mine."

Marie laughed. "Well, despite the start you gave me, I am very grateful I did not collide with your head. It looks far too large to have been comfortable."

Ha. He leaned back into the cushioned seat facing her and raised an eyebrow. "Are you implying that I have an enormous amount of conceit?"

"Because your head is so big?" she countered, her eyes sparkling mischievously at him.

"Just so."

The minx glanced away coyly. "It is my opinion that a man whose first inclination is to believe the worst of a quick comment is highly sensitive and believes himself to be exactly what he is hoping he is not."

The outrageous brat! "And what of women?"

"What of them?"

"Are they not inclined to turn a man's words into the most possible worst-case scenario and imply that they see themselves as less than they wish as well?"

"Oh, goodness no!" Marie chuckled. "You men have a tendency to say the exact thing you should not continuously. And women tend to overreact to such nonsense in the hopes of using their wiles to teach you to stop this ridiculous need to think and see things so erroneously."

Could he possibly be hearing correctly? David folded his arms while his mind raced with several compliments that the women in his life had blatantly turned into insults without him being the least able to make heads or tails of how they had concluded the worst. "It is all men's fault, then?"

"Indubitably." She covered her mouth as if she were holding back a grin. The hoyden was attempting to flummox him, and doing a very good job of it, too. David shook his head and then curiously felt his heart slowly begin to warm. If he was not careful, it would be she who was charming him, and not the other way around.

"Have you always been this ..." He paused when he could not think of the right word. What could he say that would not offend her? Women were ridiculously sensitive.

"Playful?" she asked.

That would work. "Yes."

She shrugged and looked out the window. They were heading over the bridge. "I do not know. I enjoy finding humor in everyday things. But then again, I feel most people choose to do the same."

"Do they?"

Her eyes met his, and he was struck by how startlingly blue they were. Something he had failed to notice the night before. "I would hope so," she replied. "If you cannot find joy in the oddities of life, how are you to continue on?"

His eyebrows went up. "Continue on living?"

She laughed and then bit her lip. "No. I mean, in the hope of staying positive. Seeing the world for the excitement it can bring."

"You seem to imply that we must be larking about all day long if we have any hopes of succeeding." She was a very odd girl. And such a deep conversation for this early in the morning.

"I meant no such thing." Her gaze met his again and then she surprisingly asked, "Who is your betrothed?"

His jaw dropped, and he found himself folding his arms at her abrupt nature. "I am not betrothed to anyone."

"Forgive me, Your Highness. I did not mean to upset you. I was merely hoping to ask for some advice."

"Advice? From me?"

"There is no one else around at present."

"And this advice cannot wait?" Clearly, this girl had windmills in her mind.

"Of course it can." She shook her head and turned to see more fully out the window. "Never you mind. I will keep my thoughts to myself."

For no reason at all, he began to feel a bit chastened. "We are strangers," he answered softly by way of explanation.

"Yes, and you are quite right. I should not speak of such personal things to those I do not know." Her hand clenched into a fist and then quickly hid itself beneath her skirts as she continued to look outside.

He watched the back of her head for a moment and wondered about her. No matter if she was not the person she pretended to be—she was obviously much more apprehensive than she let on. She no doubt wished to be miles away, and possibly wishing she had a friend to confide in. His mother was correct. He needed to be with her today. Perhaps he could build a sort of friendship with her. Something to help piece together what she was too afraid to say.

"My parents never betrothed me to anyone. They were hoping to wait and align a marriage that would be advantageous for the kingdom, of course, but not doing so until I was older to make the most of the match."

"A political move, then?" She looked over.

He nodded. "Something of the sort. And you? You mentioned being betrothed."

She glanced away. "Oh, well. They are merely old friends of my parents. They were hopeful of finding me a nice husband, so they sent me off on a holiday to visit with him and his family."

"Somewhere abroad?" Why would a common family send their daughter off to meet her intended in a kingdom not their own? The answer was simple. They would not. "Did your mother not accompany you?"

"She was going to at first, but now I am so grateful she stayed home!"

What a baffling comment. "Does she harp on about things, so you requested she remain behind?"

"What? No." She grinned. "Mother chose to stay home to give me time to get to know my betrothed without pressure from her."

"She seems very kind."

"Aye. She is. Too kind, really. I am much more of a nuisance to both my parents than they let on, I am sure."

And she was humble as well. Who was this girl? "You must come from a very affluent family."

Miss Marie gasped. "And why would you say that?"

He was so entranced by her surprised features, he did not answer. However, he did not need to.

"Oh, because I am traveling to meet my betrothed without my mother or father. It must seem a very strange story."

"It does. Very confusing at best." He waited a moment more before prying. "Would you like to speak of it? How you came to be here?" David was surprised to realize that he genuinely wanted to know what had happened to her. "How did you become separated from your party?"

CHAPTER SIX:

The carriage halted right then, and they both jolted a little in their seats. In two seconds, the footman was there, opening the doors. "We are at the pea fields, Your Highness. Just as you requested."

"Thank you, Charlie." David stepped from the carriage and held out his hand for Miss Marie. Her fingers clutched his as he helped her to the ground.

They had arrived at the workers' cottages, and a man in dirty clothes and gloves came out to meet them. Carlton was the overseer of all the crops their kingdom produced, though he was extremely proud of their award-winning peas. "Hallo, Your Highness. I see you made it. Your father said you would be by with another helper today."

"Yes." David brought the girl forward. "This is Miss Marie, a guest of ours for the moment. We were hoping to show her the crops and have her help out where she can."

Marie glanced over. "Am I to help do the work?"

"If you wish."

"Do you mean, pulling the weeds from the crops?"

David nodded. "Yes. Do what the workers do."

He waited for some sign of distress from her, but when she merely smiled and said, "Oh, this should be fun," he knew her dramatic performance abilities were out of his league. There was absolutely nothing fun about pulling the weeds from the crops. Nothing. Oh, how he was dreading the next few hours.

Two hours later, David was astonished at how much fun he was having. Honestly, it was as if Marie were a magical fairy full of jests. She could literally make a game from anything and everything.

"Your turn!" she called out as she tossed a handful of weed-filled mud in his direction.

"Whoa!" He stepped back as it landed with a splat at his feet. "You rascally monster! That nearly hit me."

"My apologies, Your Highness!" She laughed as though she had not one thought of forgiveness at all. "Yet it was your turn."

"It may be my turn to collect the slop and put it in the bucket, but giving me no warning whatsoever, just a shout and then hurtle—" Another large clump of muddy weeds headed straight for him. This time, he could not move fast enough, and it landed upon his shoulder. Her giggles were loud and clear. "Good gracious, woman!" He dodged just in time for the next pile to come a' flying. "Let me get the bucket first!"

"Hurry up! I thought all princes had incredible prowess when it came to sports."

Her laughter was completely contagious as David glanced over at the delightful imp. Her gloved hands were covered in grime, with splatters of it all over her face and hair. Truly, he was certain he had never seen anyone look more charming.

"Are you merely going to stand there until I hurl another chunk at you, or have you got the bucket ready? I am trying to score points here! 'Tis as if you are cheating on purpose so that I might lose."

"Cheating! You scapegrace. You infantile goat!"

"Infantile goat?" She began to giggle again. "My, your country cannot possibly be the best at wordplay, Your Highness, or you would have been able to do better than that."

He grinned as he collected the empty bucket a worker had placed next to him moments before. "And that is where you are at fault, Miss Marie. I do not have prowess or extreme wit. Unfortunately, I am completely lacking in the princely department. However, one cannot blame my country, for my father and mother have both prowess and wit in abundance. Sadly, they have produced a dunce for a son."

"Dunce?" She smiled. "Bosh! I have seen you throw. You have a very good aim. Now hold that up so I can best you this time, for I vow I will hit more weeds into the target than you have."

One of his eyebrows rose in enjoyment of the challenge. "I have to admit, you are getting better."

"I always do!" she crowed as she flung another batch of pulled weeds toward him. David lunged quickly to catch it.

"I can see." He chuckled and then hurriedly picked up a dropped bunch before she launched the next. Truth of the matter was, he loved sports—or anything outdoorsy—except weeding. Well, until today.

"You do not have to be so kind in moving to collect the piles of filth I am wildly flinging about."

"Nonsense!" He grinned. "It is obvious I am the clear winner here. Besides, it is much easier to catch them now than to pick them up later."

"'Tis true!" She tossed several more weeds his direction as they made their way down the row. "Done," she announced with a saucy grin and flick of the hair that escaped from her bonnet. "I think that is row twenty-five or twenty-six. I cannot remember."

He shook his head. "I lost count at least ten rows ago."

She glanced up at the sun and then said with that effervescent smile, "I find I quite am hungry and thirsty. How are you?"

Heavens! He had lost all track of time. "I do not think my mother expected us to be out this long. I have been having so much fun, I forgot we were working. Let us return back to the castle at once."

She pulled the gloves off her hands. "Are we not to come again? Do not forget, it is my turn to hold the bucket."

"How could I?" he asked as he held out his hand and pulled her around the plants to where he was. They began to walk back down the weeded row. He shifted the bucket to his side. "Do you work often in the fields at your home?"

"No, but I would love to." She brushed at her gown. "Though perhaps I would wear an apron if I ever did so. I hope this gown is not ruined after today."

"I doubt my mother would care."

"She is very kind."

"Is she?" He thought about her attempting to catch this delightful creature up in lies and began to wonder.

"Yes. More than I expected to a stranger like me."

He grinned down at her mud-splattered features and nudged her with his elbow. "We do not feel much like strangers now."

She paused in the middle of the crops and tilted her head as she gazed at him from beneath her bonnet. Those rosy cheeks of hers shone merrily in the sun. "No, you seem more familiar to me with each passing moment."

His heart started to beat strangely within his chest. "I am glad to hear you say that, for I am finding myself very fortunate indeed that you came to my castle for help."

Her blue eyes dimmed a bit. "Do you feel fortunate? I am not putting you or your family out?"

"Of course not. How could we feel put upon with such happiness around us?"

She looked over the land and then nodded. "Your kingdom is a very happy one."

When her gaze met his again, he said simply, "I was referring to you."

CHAPTER SEVEN:

"Mother, I have never seen anything like it. She handled the pea farm with energy and enthusiasm as if pulling weeds in the mud was second nature to her." David whirled on his heel in front of the queen. They were in her immaculate personal sitting room and she was perched upon the chaise lounge, the skirts of her mint-green gown puddling upon the floor beneath her.

"Do you mean to say she enjoyed herself?" His mother shook her head in disbelief.

"Not only enjoyed herself, but she created a game of the thing." He continued, "Do not doubt when I share that she had me laughing nearly the whole time. I did not want it to end."

His mother leaned forward. "Are you trying to tell me that I send a girl out weeding and she not only enjoys herself doing the task, but has everyone else joining in her larks too?"

He shrugged. "Yes. I supposed that is what happened. It was simply enchanting."

"No, dearest. The word you mean to use is 'baffling.'"

"That as well." He grinned shyly and then revealed, "Whatever it is, I find I quite like it. She is extremely enjoyable."

"Is she?" The queen folded her arms. "And did you learn anything of her past today?"

"No. Nothing new, though she is beginning to trust me."

She waved her hand. "What an odd little creature. First, we are certain she is royalty, but now she has proven to be at such ease with weeding the pea fields, perhaps I was mistaken. Perhaps she is not royalty at all. And if she is not royalty, what is she?"

"I have no idea." David felt his heart warm again. "Though I am nearly convinced she has done nothing untoward. It cannot be in her nature to be harmful to anyone, I suspect." He met his mother's gaze, but quickly looked away.

"Did she send off the letter to her family? Did anyone see where in Dillany she addressed the envelope?"

"I sent Albert in to fetch it for her, but I must confess, it slipped my mind to have him bring it to you first. I did not see the letter myself."

"David!" His mother stared at him as if she were in shock. "How could you have done something so foolish? I specifically asked that all mail go through me or your father until we ascertain what the girl is up to."

"Do not be cross. It has been a rather long day. Albeit, a very fun day, but long nonetheless. I was no doubt taking a quick snooze when it all happened."

She stood up and put her hands on her hips. "Either you were or you were not. To imply that you do not know, when you were the one to send Albert in, seems as though you are attempting to hide something from me."

"I told Albert to see that her letter was sent and then fell asleep. It was as simple as that."

"Well, you completely ruined every hope I had of finding out who this girl is!"

He sighed and sat down upon a wooden chair against the wall. "Does it matter overly much if we do not find out?"

She blinked. "She is lost, David. Yes, it matters who she is."

"You know what I am referring to."

"No, I do not believe I do. In fact, the whole of this conversation is beginning to vex me completely," she huffed. "Now, please remove yourself and find the chit and hopefully gain a bit more knowledge than you have at the moment. I want this settled as soon as possible. If she is some common hoyden, we need to know it immediately before you embarrass yourself and the family by becoming smitten with her charms."

David smiled at her twisted logic. "Are you implying that I need to spend more time with Miss Marie and gain her trust before I spend too much time with her and find myself in love?"

"Ooh." She fluttered her hands and sat back down. "Do not attempt to make me see reason at this moment. I am clearly too upset to think properly. Just find out who she is, please. And soon."

"Very well, Mother." He bowed and headed toward the door. "I will do precisely as you ask, though there are absolutely no promises I can make in regards to falling in love with the delightful creature."

"David!" she gasped as he closed the door behind him. "David! Come back here at once."

He merely smiled as he strode down the long hallway, past the staircase to the east wing, and into the library, where he knew Miss Marie was curled upon a sofa, reading.

CHAPTER EIGHT:

Kyra looked up as Prince David came into the library, and her stomach did an odd little flip. Suddenly, she began to feel fluttery and slightly nervous. "Hello, Your Highness." She smiled, hoping he could not see the silliness she was exuding.

He paused near the settee where she sat. "Hello."

She waited for him to say something, but he did not, only stared down at her.

"Yes?" Her nerves got the better of her, and she could feel a giggle rising.

He shook his head and then sat down on a high-backed chair opposite her and leaned forward. "I have no idea why I am here, so do not ask me."

"Very well."

He bit his lip and then looked charmingly at her. "Forgive me—how is your book? Am I intruding?"

Prince David seemed like the least remorseful person she had ever seen. "'Tis a good book, but I welcome your company anyway," she responded politely as she folded the pages and placed it upon the small table to her right.

He reached over with his long arm and snatched it up. "*The Lily and the Toad*," he read aloud. "I do not think I have ever come across this novel before." Flipping it from side to side, he asked, "It *is* a novel, I presume?"

"Yes, though I fear it is something akin to a fairy tale my mother used to read to me when I was a wee little one."

"Your mother?" He glanced up at her. "Your mother can read?"

Kyra looked away and then told a great fib, not quite meeting his eye. "Why, yes, everyone in my kingdom can read. We are taught when we are young."

"Even you?"

She nodded toward the book. "As you can see."

He smiled. "Excuse me—I am a dolt sometimes. Of course you can read. I was taught as well, but I do not think my kingdom has been educated. However, I did not think to question you when you first came in here, merely accepting your reading for what it was. And now, I find myself too inquisitive by half. I beg your pardon. Sometimes my nature forces me to ask ridiculous questions and appear foolish."

Kyra wondered at such a speech. Why, the prince seemed utterly quick to excuse himself, so much so that it was plainly obvious he wished to know who she was and how she came to be here. She took a deep breath and clasped her hands together. "Forgive me. I know I am being exceptionally vague and that must come off excessively rudely to you and your family, but I fear I cannot trust anyone at this time. Not even the nicest hosts I have ever come across." At least they pretended to be very nice. She would never tell him what she really thought.

His jaw dropped slightly before he covered the action by rubbing his chin. He started and stopped as though he wished to say something a good minute or so before he finally asked, "And how may I gain your trust,

Miss Marie? I find that I wish to know more of you, but have not the least notion of how to do so."

Kyra fidgeted in her seat, suddenly knowing full well why he was here. "'Tis not you who wants to know of me—your mother and father sent you here to woo me, did they not? You are supposed to be kind to extract whatever information you can."

He leaned back and crossed his ankles. "How am I to answer such an accusation?"

"By dodging the question with your own aimed back at me, I suppose." One eyebrow rose. "However, it only fuels my suspicions more."

"Your suspicions?" He seemed flabbergasted. "You happen to be the only person who has any answers at all. I find it extremely presumptuous that you would use thinly veiled sarcasm to imply that we are not supposed to be suspicious of a person we have taken under our wing and literally sheltered from the storm. Is it not our right and duty to quiz a person about who they are and how they came to be in our home?"

Kyra stood up, and instantly, the prince scrambled to his feet as well. Then without another word, she walked from the room. Whether or not he was right, she certainly owed him nothing. Yes, they might be curious about who she was, but this was her welfare they were battling about. Not his. Make no mistake, it was her horse from the wreckage that came into their stables the evening before. She had no idea how they came about acquiring Lightning. And there was no way of knowing if his kingdom was behind the catastrophe. As she burst from the room, she could feel her hands beginning to shake.

All this time, she had held herself together and kept her emotions in check, but now it was too much. After turning the wrong way once, she was able to correct herself and find the main passage that led to the back gardens of the castle. One of the footmen opened the door for her, and she took a large gulp of fresh air as she headed toward the central hedged garden. After she had sent her letter, she had found this darling hidden spot and had spent several minutes upon a bench attempting to remain positive in the light of this very precarious predicament.

With only a few twists and turns, she found the secluded bench once more and curled up on it, as if she were a little girl on her father's grounds. Kyra put her feet up, making sure her gown properly covered her ankles, and then placed her arms on her knees. This time, she was not so brave and optimistic as before.

There was absolutely no reason for this nonsense, but she suddenly felt very much alone. She needed help—desperately needed help—yet knew everything hung upon what would happen here. Of course they wanted to know her story. Of course they were curious. Prince David and his family no doubt knew she was royalty by the way he questioned her.

Kyra groaned and laid her head upon her arms. Why was she so stupid to believe they would not find out? She had most likely been giving off signs the whole time and did not know it. How *could* she know it? She had rarely been around commoners to understand their mannerisms compared to her own. And the reading! How did she not see that as a giveaway?

She wished she could like this kingdom. They seemed kind—yet how could she trust them? Writing that letter had been the hardest thing she had done. It took every ounce of strength to recount in detail how scared she had been the night before, the gunshots, and her fears without shedding a tear. Every single ounce. And yet, right now, with the scant pressure she had received from a concerned prince, she could feel her anxiety rise.

First one tear and then another frustrating tear fell. She wanted to be home. She did not wish to be anywhere near here. She was never good at lies and playacting—it was all too much. No. She wished she had never gone to meet her betrothed. Had she stayed home, none of this would have happened.

"Miss Marie?" the prince called from nearby.

Good heavens, he would be upon her in a moment. She wiped at her eyes and sat up straight. Just as she was going to call out in answer, he turned the corner. Their gazes collided, and for a moment, neither one moved. If she did not know better, she would assume he was genuinely worried for her. His stricken face said more about his character than any action could have in that bit of time. And then he spoke.

"I deeply apologize for my words earlier. I did not mean to offend you."

He did not take a step toward her, and yet—"You are sincere."

"Of course I am sincere. Despite not knowing much about you, I fear I worry greatly over what you will not reveal. And yet, I do not wish to offend you or force you to believe you are in danger in anyway because you are not. I promise you this much, you are completely safe here."

"However, you do not trust me. You do not trust the words that I speak, and therefore are as cautious of me as I am of you," she replied.

CHAPTER NINE:

"I cannot stop you from keeping your secrets. I would never force anything from you. But when a person is shrouded in mystery it does naturally create several complications." David took a deep breath and went on. "However, when I watch you run from me and wish distance between us, because of my attempts to lure you into conversation, I find I would much rather have a friend, even confidant, who I knew nothing of, than to have a stranger who wanted nothing to do with me."

Kyra turned more fully toward him. "I do not mean to be so mysterious. I wish more than anything to be able to confide in someone. But, I dare not."

"May I?" He pointed to the space on the bench next to her.

Kyra hesitated, her heart strangely beating, before moving even more over. "Yes."

He came and sat next to her and the sudden awareness of him so very close only added to her confusion. "Can I ask you something?" he asked.

She let out a sort of frantic chuckle. "Have you not been asking questions?"

He grinned. "I supposed so. But this one, I promise not to reveal the answer to anyone—least of all my parents."

Intrigued she flicked a glance his way. "And what is that?"

"I was wondering if Marie was your real name. You do not have to answer with your real name, I am only curious to see if it is."

"Does Marie not sound common enough for you?" She chuckled more easily this time.

"Yes, that is the problem."

"The problem?" When he did not answer she said, "No. Well, it is my second name."

He nodded slowly and then his eyes met hers with a seriousness she had yet to see before. He rose one hand and gently pushed away a strand of hair upon her brow. "I am finding it my dearest wish to one day know what your true name is."

The closeness, his fingertips, his deep voice, those eyes—it was all doing unimaginable things to her breathing. And a small part of her begged that she faced the truth and answer him. "I hope one day you will." There. It was done. She had betrayed her betrothed and suddenly she felt a smidge freer than she had a moment before.

David continued to stare at her before gently moving his hand to the back of her head and pulling her forward. His lips came to rest upon her forehead for a brief second and he whispered, "Thank you."

Kyra had never felt so overwhelmed, or so willing to close her eyes and run her nose and mouth along his jaw. She quickly pulled back before she lost all of her reserve and did just what she wished. Her father would more than likely dispose of the prince if he had learned of any of this. She looked at the hedge in front of her and whispered, "This maze reminds me so much of life. Every twist, every turn—even every halt and wrong path, they all represent the roads we travel."

"You are very philosophical at the moment." He leaned back and straightened his legs in front of him. "What brings this on?"

"I do not know exactly. Perhaps you, this place. All of it."

He nodded. "It is very enchanting."

She took a deep breath and inhaled the smell of roses. They must be nearer the rose garden than she thought. "Yes, there is something about your kingdom that invites you to stay awhile and enjoy it here."

"Do you wish to stay here longer?"

She shook her head. "No. Not at all. I want to go home more than anything."

His eyebrows rose. "Then why mention it?"

"Because I feel the tug to stay nonetheless. Tis very disconcerting to know you are needed elsewhere and wish to be somewhere else, yet long to be here too."

He smirked and waggled an eyebrow. "Are you certain it has nothing to do with your growing fondness of me?"

"You? Ha. Why would I be growing fond of you?"

"Because I am handsome."

She laughed. "There are handsome men everywhere. I desire much more than a pretty face to attract me."

"Very well." He pretended to pout. "But you have got to admit that it certainly helps that I am handsome."

She nudged him with her elbow. "Your conceit knows no bounds."

"None at all."

Suddenly she wished nothing more than to kiss that smug look off of his face. "And what would you do with me, if you could have me?" she challenged. "I am way too headstrong by half to be bullied by the likes of you."

"Good Heavens woman! You have me bullying you already."

"Why not? You are convinced I want to remain here because of your good looks."

David became more serious. "Nay. I am convinced you want to stay here because you feel the same pull as I do." He glanced away. "But neither of us can build anything upon a false foundation."

"Why must we build something? Why can we not merely get to know one another?"

He looked at her for a long moment and then said, "Very well, and what do you enjoy doing when you are not captivating the hearts of princes?"

Her heart flipped, but she quickly hid her reaction. "The only thing your heart is captivated over is yourself." And then she quickly continued lest he try to answer her. "I enjoy doing all the things a young lady must. Needlework, sewing, watercolor, and taking long walks outside."

"What? No horse riding? No adventures? You do not seem the type to me. I picture you chasing sunsets and galloping through daydreams."

She laughed with him. "What a fanciful picture of me. I think I rather like it."

"Do you?" Their gazes caught again and she could not help but notice the way he managed to make her heart flip topsy-turvy. She looked away coyly, attempting to tamp down the unnecessary complication of this attraction between them. "You know, I did love to wear my poofy dresses and climb the trees in the apple orchard. I would zoom clear to the top and then gaze out at the world below me."

"And what did you dream of way up there?"

You. She stopped herself before uttering the words and instead remembered the many, many hours she spent daydreaming of finding a handsome prince to share her dreams with and laugh with. "I do not remember overly much," she whispered.

He tilted his head and gave her a funny look. "Oddly enough I do not believe you."

"Very well." She could feel her cheeks turning red. "I dreamed of what life would be like when I married someday."

"Honestly?" He grinned. "Is that what girls imagine when they are alone? Of life when they are older and married."

"Of course. What did you dream of?"

He shrugged. "The buck I would catch on my next bow hunt."

Her jaw dropped. "Of all the horrendous—" Kyra could not help herself, she began to giggle. "Boys are so very much different than girls."

"Oh, I do not think so. Not as we get older." Those eyes found hers again. "Now all I wonder about is what life would be like with you."

CHAPTER TEN:

David whistled as he jauntily made his way down the large castle hallways. Truly he was not sure if he could get any happier at that moment. He grinned as he recalled the drop of Miss Marie's jaw and the faint blush upon her cheeks at his declaration of thinking of her. She was an angel. A mysterious angel with a troubled past, but an angel nonetheless.

He did not give one fig what his mother or father felt about the girl. There was no way she had an evil bone in her body. Her fear and lack of trust must have stemmed from something she witnessed or saw, not because of anything she had done. David would bet his life upon it.

"David!" his mother trilled behind him.

He turned and paused as she rushed to catch up, her breathing much more pronounced. "Come into the blue drawing room." She waved with her hand and sailed past him into the room to his right. Once he followed she nodded to the awaiting footmen to close the door.

David's chest felt the slightest smidgeon of unease as he sat down upon the chair nearest the window. "What has happened?" he asked.

She looked shocked. "Why I have been hoping to ask the same thing. Several of the staff have indicated that you went to the maze with Miss Marie and were there for some time. Now you are whistling like a loon in the hallways. Tell me what have you discovered? Is she as wicked as we thought? Was she involved in the disturbing wreckage our soldiers found?"

"Good heavens, Mother. Anyone would think you were eager to discover the worst in people. You almost seem gleeful."

She huffed and sat down in the matching chair next to him. "Do not be that way, David. I am not gleeful, just merely eager to see if my first observations were correct."

He leaned back in his chair and sat his hands upon his lap. "Well, I do not believe we have anything to worry about over Miss Marie. She is a delightful creature and though she has been frightened, I personally do not believe she has done any harm to anyone. Least of all that wreckage. If the two are related—which I doubt—I am certain she will have had nothing to with the damage and may very well turn out to be the one whose carriage was attacked." He hoped not. Oh, how his chest ached at the thought of terror she must be feeling within his own lands.

His mother folded her arms. "And you believe you have uncovered all of this while speaking with her just now?"

"Yes."

"Learned all of what? There is nothing here but speculation, my son. I still believe she must be tested."

"Why? What more could you possibly put the girl through? Can you not see that she is clearly not a threat or danger to us?"

"Do you know her name? Do you know where she is from? Can you give me any actual fact about this girl that states why she is hiding from us?"

David sighed. "No. Not any real fact. Merely that she is fearful to reveal anything to us."

"Fearful?" She shook her head. "The basis for the safety of our kingdom is based upon her being fearful? No. I will not accept such lax conclusions, even from you, my dear. We need to ascertain whether she is royalty or not."

"I believe she very well may be."

His mother shot him a look. "You believe she may be? Or are you hoping she is?"

He shrugged. "Whether she is or not, does not signify. For I truly believe she is innocent in this all."

A shrewd eye passed over his features before his mother declared, "Or she has hoodwinked you." She tapped her finger upon her mouth. "No, I must think of another test to put her through. Something more clever than the last." She stood up and began to pace in front of him. "You said she made the most of working in the pea fields as though she belonged there. Do not forgot that statement of yours. It proves more than anything the importance of this next test."

"And just what have you planned for her, Mother?" David could feel a slight tension in his neck.

"Hush. I am thinking now." She took a few steps and then paused as her eyes scanned the fields through the window behind him. "It must be something only royalty would know."

David watched his mother with a growing sense of dread beginning to form. What if she found out Miss Marie was indeed not good for the kingdom? Could he accept such a reality? Would his heart survive being duped so well?

"Aha!" She flipped on her heel and began to pace again. "I have just the thing. It is so brilliant, I am amazed I did not think of it sooner."

"What?" He slowly sat forward. "What misery will you put this girl through now?"

"No. Not misery." His mother grinned. "It will be much subtler than that." She halted and turned fully toward him. "I shall simply give her the spoon test."

"The what?"

"It will be in the peas. Do you not see?" She began to grow more excited by the moment. "It is simply the perfect answer. How will Miss Marie eat her peas for dinner tomorrow?"

He was certain his mother had gone mad. "And how will eating one's peas prove anything?"

She placed her hands upon her hips and grinned like a loon. "No common house would have a spoon with their dinnerware. It is only the royalty who are afforded such luxuries, since the invention of the thing."

He rubbed his hands over his face. "And if she eats the peas with her fork, you will send her packing?"

"Possibly. I cannot have you falling in love with a commoner. One who is obviously attempting to be someone she is not to hide a mysterious past."

David took a deep breath and nodded his head slowly. "And if she eats with a spoon?"

Then I will know she is a distressed princess who needs our help. Either way, she will never be truly worthy enough to be crowned a princess in over our land."

He stood up as a flash of anger coursed through him. "And why is that? If she is royalty, why could I not choose to wed her?"

His mother took a step toward him. Her finger going to his chest. "I knew it. I knew you had fallen head over heels for the girl. Now, more than ever I must prove that she is indeed worthy of you. For I refuse to give you up to anyone less than royalty."

"So you will insist on pea test to prove if she is indeed worthy enough to become the Princess of Peas?" he spat out.

That smug grin grew to a full blown smile. "Of course. And you will be certain to stay away from her until dinner. No cheating. No telling her anything."

"Of course not, Mother," David said. "Why would I dream of disrupting any plan of yours?" Though she was wrong about one thing. If he felt Miss Marie was the girl for him, no one would stop him from wedding her. No one. Not even her betrothed.

CHAPTER ELEVEN:

The next day for lunch, Kyra came down to the dining room dressed in a light green gown and her stomach grumbling. She had not been this hungry for some time and everything smelled delicious. David and his father stood as she entered the room and remained standing until the footman pushed her in the chair up to the table.

It was only a few seconds before the queen entered in a blue summer gown and the process was repeated with the men standing. Kyra remained seated as was custom. Though once everyone was sat at the table, then the chattering began.

"And how have you fared, Miss Marie?" the queen asked as she busied herself with placing a napkin upon her lap.

Kyra did the same. "Do you mean here at your castle?"

"Of course." The king smiled. "We would like to be aware of anything amiss for those we host. And we hope your stay has been pleasant."

The bed was atrociously odd and one could barely sleep upon its stacked mattress. Her hosts and servants were bound and determined to fish as much information out of her as they could. And their son was attempting, nay winning, in making her as completely flustered and confused as he most definitely could. She was positive her heart would never be the same. And thinking of her heart, she could not but help remember the tears she shed for her servants and longing for the family she missed last night and again this morning. But all in all, considering the circumstances, she supposed it could be much worse. "Thank you, you are too kind. I am enjoying myself very much."

The king and queen both nodded and smiled, then turned their attention to the course of cooked peas being brought into the room.

Kyra had a fondness for cooked peas and had since she was a wee little girl. Her grandpapa had taught her how to take her fork and stack the little peas down the prongs and then slide them off with her lips into her mouth. Something her mother would mourn over.

"Kyra, if you insist on eating your peas like a commoner, I would have you removed from this table immediately," would usually be the response.

And Kyra would most always retort with, "But grandpapa the king taught me how!"

"Yes, but your grandfather in not the best example of manners, my dear, and you know it."

Kyra grinned and picked up her fork, remembering all of the silliness she and her grandpapa would get into before he passed on.

She glanced up and it would seem the whole room was watching her with the fork. Indeed, David, his parents and even the servants were looking right at her. Kyra quickly dropped the thing. How bad of manners was it to hold a fork while eating peas anyway? She quickly picked up the spoon her mother had always insisted on and scooped up a few peas. Then looked up again. No one seemed to have moved an inch. Were they waiting for her to sample a bite?

"Is something amiss?" she asked, now growing ever worried. Had they poisoned her peas, or something? Why was everyone waiting for her?

"No." The queen chuckled. "Pardon me, I was merely waiting to see if you enjoyed the peas."

Er..? Suddenly Kyra felt very suspicious. "Why?"

"Because it is what our land is known for," the king bragged as he took a scoop in his mouth.

Oh. That would make sense. They were eager to see if she liked what they produced. Why was she being such a ninny? She took a sigh of relief and slipped the spoon in her mouth. And then another and then another. "These peas are the most delicious peas I have ever tasted."

"Are they?" The queen's smug smile appeared out of place. "That is good to know."

Kyra glanced back at her spoon and then up at them. It was then that she caught David's eye. He was not merely smiling; it would seem as if he would burst from some inner excitement.

"Has something happened I was not aware of?"

The king looked between David and her. "David?"

When the prince looked over the king shook his head slightly. "You need to be wise, my son. And very sure before you decide anything."

The queen tittered. "And why talk about this now? Let us all partake of our luncheon and then afterward we should chat." She looked directly at Kyra. "Do you not think so, your highness?"

"Of course," Kyra sputtered, not certain what was going on.

The king raised his glass and set it right back down again. The bottom rim clipped his plate and the red liquid spilled everywhere.

Suddenly the whole room began a flurry of busyness as the servants rushed to and fro. In a flash, the tablecloth was replaced and so was the king's drink. And then just as quickly the second course was served.

After the servants settled, an uneasy quiet came over the room.

"What did you say?" the king asked her.

"Me?" She asked in shock. "I did not say a thing."

"No, before I spilled my drink. The reason I spilled it. What did you say?"

She had to think back a bit. "I believe I was agreeing with the queen." Should she not have? Was he angry at her? Slowly her hungry stomach began to twist in knots.

"It was subconscious," David broke in.

"Yes, I realize that." The king leaned toward her. "What are your parents' names, your highness? What kingdom are you from?"

How did he know? Had she given it away?

"What is wrong?" the queen asked. "Is it such a dreadful secret to hide behind the rouse of commoner? We know who you are now."

Without knowing what else to do, Kyra stood up. Suddenly she felt very alone and trapped. Could she honestly trust them? Did she dare?

"There is no need for this." The queen motioned for the men not to stand up, and then she pointed to the chair. "Let us chat once the meal is over. I am sure you have much you would like to tell me."

"Forgive me, your majesties." She glanced back and forth between the two of them desperately attempting to think of a good enough excuse. "I am not feeling very well at the moment. I think I need to lie down."

"Miss Marie, wait," David called to her as she walked toward the door.

Two footman stepped in front of the exit and blocked her path.

"You do not have permission to leave this room until we allow it," answered the king.

Kyra's chest began to pound. "Please, I need to leave this moment."

David stood up. "This is ridiculous. Let her go. She is obviously in distress."

Her eyes met his and he continued, "What does it matter who she is? Miss Marie came to us for help and now that you have ascertained she is royalty, there is nothing more you could wish to know."

His mother clearly was not used to be thwarted. "David, sit down at once. This has become quite the farce all of the sudden. And forgive me, Miss Marie, you are welcome to leave. However, we will continue this conversation and I do ask that you treat me with enough civility to answer *all* of my questions."

The footmen parted and Kyra did not hesitate as she rushed into the hallway with the queen's parting words sneaking out and capturing the frantic pounding of her heart.

"It is for your own good David." She could hear the queen say. "If you have fallen in love with the girl, we must know who she is!"

There it was again, that feeling of glee and dread all at the same time.

CHAPTER TWELVE:

Kyra ran down the long corridors and out into the garden once more. It was a bright summer evening; the sun would still shine for an hour or so yet. The family believed she was in her room, but she needed something more private than that, something without maids. She needed to think and plan and mostly she needed to halt these ridiculous feelings that have surfaced.

Fear. Guilt. Pain. Hope. Longing. Joy.

She was a complete and utter mess of a princess. And everything here was coming on too quickly. She had never known anyone like David before. Heaven knew her heart could not contain itself when he was near. But was it love? Was that what it felt like? This fearful, wild unknown path. She longed so very much to reveal everything to him, and could truly believe he was earnest and honest with her. Yet, his parents. Where they overbearing to be protective of him, or did they have their own malicious reasons?

She sat down upon her favorite bench and brought her feet up, very unladylike, and tucked her head into her knees. Taking a few deep breaths, she attempted to sort out the muddle within. More than anything she missed her family. How she wished someone was here who could advise her. Someone to see this from the outside perspective and tell her what a silly goose she was. But they were not here. No one was.

As always, whenever she thought of home, her thoughts turned to the servants she had lost. What had become of them? Were they well? Had they made their way back to the kingdom? Were they all dead?

Kyra closed her eyes. Her father would solve all of these mysteries for her. She knew he would. As soon as he arrived. Yet, having only sent the letter the day before, it could be nightfall tomorrow before he arrived. And the queen has vowed to speak with her and expects her to answer any question she asks.

Fear shuddered down her spine at the thought. The anxiety at such an interview was not helpful.

The sun dipped a little lower, and Kyra blinked into its fading light. There was home. To the west. Slowly Kyra put first one foot down and then the other. With the sun right there, she easily knew her way home, or at least could get far enough away to make progress and perhaps intercept her father tomorrow. Even if the queen said she was not to leave, who was to stop her? Certainly if she approached the stables as if she were about to go riding, no one would think otherwise. Or would they?

Kyra jumped from the bench and made her way back toward the castle. It was worth the effort to try, anyhow. It was time she went for a ride.

CHAPTER THIRTEEN:

As she wound her way through the labyrinth of the castle hallways, she began to plan her escape. Earlier, it had not taken much to convince Prince David that he looked exhausted after their excursion so that she could write and—most importantly—send her letter in peace, but this might take a little more planning. Dinner was at eight o'clock. That meant she would most likely not be missed for a few hours at least. Her heart began to pound in excitement as she raced into her room and searched the wardrobe for suitable riding attire.

There in the back, the thoughtful queen had not only supplied her with a nice riding dress, but she also added a studier pair of boots, a crop, and a bonnet, too. The boots were slightly too big, but all in all, the outfit did not look half bad. She turned from side to side in the looking glass as she adjusted her heavier dark-blue skirts.

Kyra took a deep breath, gave herself a nod in the mirror, and then glanced around the rest of the room. It had been tidied by the maid hours ago. Besides her shoes, there was really nothing here for her to bring back home anyway. If she stayed to the edges of the road and hid when anyone was coming, perhaps she would not be noticed. Her only disadvantage was lack of food, but it did not matter. Her kingdom was merely two days' ride, if she went quickly enough, and she roughly knew where to find water for her and the horse.

She grinned as the excitement in her began to intensify. It was now or never. Kyra tiptoed out of the guestroom and made it down the hall toward the side doors of the castle—the opposite of where she had been, and by the stables. Her plan was flawless, except for one minor detail—Prince David might be worried about her.

"There you are!" the devilish man called as he hurried toward her. "Where are you off to? The maids said you never retired to your room. I have been searching the whole place over and could never find you to apologize for my family."

She had to think quickly. Already he was eyeing her riding clothes. "I went to the hedged garden to think, and then decided to go for a ride. Would—would you like to join me?" Her only chance of escape now was to outrun him. Blast it.

"I would love to. 'Tis the perfect time for such an outing, right when the earth begins to cool, yet it is still not too cold. Will you wait a moment while I change into riding gear?"

"Yes, of course. I will be in the stables."

He nodded. "Very good. I will have my man be certain to make sure the lads wait upon you and that they know we are riding together."

"You are too kind, Your Highness." She had not thought that the stable hands might not let her go. Good heavens. How she missed her own home where she could simply do whatever she wished, when she wished it. Within reason, of course. This place had her under lock and key.

As Kyra stepped out into the courtyard that led to the stables, she looked around once more at the layout of the area. It looked so completely different in the daylight without the storm clouds. She found the sun shining above the distant hills, and knew those hills would lead her home. Her eyes focused on the pea fields in front of the mountains, and though they beckoned her to stay and play within them again, the call to return home was much stronger.

By the time she reached the stables, she was ready to leave once more, and was even wondering if she would be able to slip away before the prince returned. The men were not hesitant to borrow a saddle for Thunder and even helped her up as she clutched her gown, being sure not to show her muslin petticoats. "Tell the prince I will be heading west toward the pea fields." She smiled down at one of the lads, who was clutching a rather large rooster.

"Certainly, miss. If I had a scrap of paper, I'd write him a note, except my penmanship isn't the best. And I don't know all them words, neither." The rooster squirmed, and the lad dropped him. The rascal went scurrying around the door and into the barn. "Never mind him—he's always gettin' into the barn. He likes the hay. He should be in his coop, but he likes it in here."

The young man seemed nice enough and not the type who would overturn a coach, but one never knew. "Thank you." She nodded and then turned to leave, but her crop got caught on her white stocking. Thunder fretted a bit as she removed the crop, and then with a tilt of her hat, she managed to get them both out of the stables and through the courtyard without any more mishaps.

Kyra sighed in relief as the guards merely waved her across the bridge. Was it truly this easy to leave? She had the horse slow to a slight walk so as not to bump into anyone else coming up. There were not a ton of people around, but a few with wares. One particular cart looked to be brimming full to the top with lavender. The queen must surely love the herb for there to be that much.

As she headed toward the end of the bridge, Kyra experienced a bit of uncertainty on which way to go. The prince was sure to follow her to the west, yet she knew that if she headed to the east, there would be trouble afoot. Or at least, the definite possibility of trouble.

Kyra pulled the wide-brimmed hat lower on her brow to conceal her features and then plunged on and headed west. With a bit of luck, she would be able to canter out of the village soon and be far from the prince's sight before he caught up with her.

It was an easy trot through the streets of the village, dodging happy people and fascinating sights of families laughing and speaking with one another. She could tell this kingdom was peaceful. Perhaps as peaceful and kind as their royal family appeared to be.

She pushed away several despicable thoughts and instead allowed herself a little daydream of the life this kingdom must live, if indeed they truly were a kind king and queen.

CHAPTER FOURTEEN:

"Which way did she say she was going?" David's heart twisted in his chest as a feeling of dread came over him. Why would Miss Marie leave without him? Did she not know there were bandits afoot?

"She said she was heading in the direction of the pea fields, Your Highness."

David looked at the young man and then nodded. He felt a bit more at ease. Perhaps she was merely returning to their spot from early that morning. "Thank you, Paul." Without another thought, he spurred his horse through the courtyard and across the bridge. The few people left upon the structure quickly scurried out of his way and bowed before him. He nodded to his subjects as he passed, hopefully not appearing too rude, and then rode on through the village and out toward the road that led to the wide expanse of crops.

The girl could not have more than a scant ten minutes' head start, could she? How long had it taken him to dress while she got the horse saddled? He spurred his horse on and quickened the pace. He should be able to reach her without too much trouble.

Except after riding hard a good fifteen minutes or so, he still had not caught up with her. And she was nowhere to be found in the fields they had visited earlier. He would have been able to see her horse for quite a ways had she been out there, but she was not.

He reined in and slowed down, attempting to imagine where Miss Marie could have gone. Would she have attempted to return home? Yet why would she flee? Would she not feel more comfortable in the castle, waiting for her parents to fetch her? Or was she not telling the truth? Was she actually behind the wreckage his men had come upon? Each passing minute that he did not stumble upon her, he became a slight bit more worried. Darkness would not fall upon them until after nine, but goodness, she was not hoping to travel these roads until dark, was she? Why did the cursed girl not stay where he could keep her safe?

Botheration! David growled under his breath as he crested a hill. He could see the end of his kingdom about ten miles beyond. There was a great lake that bordered the territory and the other nation nearest. He halted and peered out toward the lake, enjoying for a moment the breathtaking beauty below him. And then his eyes followed the road leading around the lake. It was there at the farthest bend leading into the next kingdom that he could make out the small figure. It was too large to be a lone figure walking—someone must be riding a horse.

Marie! Where was she going? And alone like this! He immediately set his horse into motion and began to descend the hill, his eyes never leaving the figure. Then he saw two more shapes burst from the edge of the lake and surround the single one. They blurred together to form a larger mass until the two figures broke away and then split in two, leaving no trace of the first form. What had he witnessed? She was gone. Had someone swooped in and carried her off just like that?

Instantly, he urged his horse into a gallop and rode as hard and fast as he could, his heartbeat quickening by the second. Had he really witnessed what he thought he had? What if it was not Miss Marie at all? What if all three of the figures had been riding together, and he simply had not noticed them?

But if that were the case, why did they spring out of the forest like that, and then why did they divert themselves off the road? No, it was a kidnapping he had witnessed—he was sure of it. Even if it was not Miss Marie, someone was in trouble and needed his help, and he refused to allow ruffians such liberties in his land. No, they would pay, and they would pay dearly.

CHAPTER FIFTEEN:

Kyra yelped in fright as two large men burst from the edge of the wood and surrounded her. She attempted to move out of their reach, but poor Thunder was as frightened as she was and reared up instead. Kyra held on tightly to the reins and hair of the horse, but her sidesaddle was not up to the feat, and she flew into one of the men's arms as soon as the beast rose up.

She fought and pummeled and shouted as loudly and fiercely as she could, but could not best the great brawn of the brute who was holding her.

"Quiet!" he growled as he grabbed her arms and forced her to sit in front of him on the saddle. "If you do not behave, I will cut out your tongue." For emphasis, he held one large arm around her, pinning her limbs to her sides, and removed a large knife from its sheath.

Kyra flinched back, but was even then calculating the amount of time it would take to release herself from the man's hold and remove the knife from his grasp. "You would not dare cut out my tongue!" she snarled back.

The other man laughed. "You better watch yourself, Rundle. That feline hasn't taken her eyes away from your knife since you pulled it out, and she don't seem as much afraid of it as she should be."

"Best be getting off this road anyway before someone finds us."

At that moment, Kyra lunged and kicked with her knee, flipping the knife out of her captor's hand and to the ground.

"What the devil?" he snarled as she slipped from his grasp and tumbled to the road. She immediately dove for the knife, not minding the horses' hooves, but the other man was quicker.

He snatched it up and then pointed the thing right at her. "Get back up on that saddle now." He pointed to her horse with the knife. "If you're too stubborn to do this easily, we'll see that you behave."

Her father had taught her never to show fear, and in this instance, she knew that once she left the road, things would not fare well. "I cannot climb up into this saddle on my own! Are you daft?"

He walked over and threw her up on it, his knife slicing painfully across her forearm as he did so.

"There! Ye happy now? Oh, looky! Did the big bad knifey cut you?"

Kyra looked down, but refused to focus on the stream of blood she could feel running down her elbow. Instead, she clutched her gown and wrapped it around the wound. "Mock me again, and you will live to regret it."

"She doesn't just look like her—she even speaks as if she's the princess we've been searching for!" the first man said. "Too high and mighty for her own good."

"Well, let's get off this road, then, and be gone with the brat afore someone comes looking for her. We can ask all the questions we want later."

"You are fools!" she hissed as the man grabbed her reins and hauled the horse forward. "Prince David of

Haltaen Court was coming to meet me, and when he does, you will both die for what you are attempting to do."

"Oh, is the little prince going to hurt us?" The other man laughed.

"I was merely pointing out that as soon as that distraction happens, you will live to regret the day you were born. If I were a princess, would I be riding out here alone?" She attempted a laugh. "Nodcocks! I am one of the castle guards, and you shall regret the moment you laid eyes upon me, for I shall destroy you both. I am merely following you now because I have nothing better to do."

"Foolish girl! You are following us because your arm is cut and we have you hostage. Castle guard, indeed! What a tale you can spin!"

They moved off the path and followed a hidden trail into the woods. She attempted another tactic while counting the seconds they traveled from the road in hopes she could make it back. "Who are you looking for, anyway? And why must you go after a helpless princess? Can you not fight something bigger and stronger, or are you afraid?"

"Listen to her chatter on as if she owns the place! Right pain in the neck, if you ask me."

"Princess or no, Codwig, we should bop her over the head and leave her to bleed in the road."

"That's what we should do. Good one."

Kyra yawned as she clutched the bandage on her arm tighter. "If this is supposed to intimidate me, it doesn't. At all. In fact, I am not certain either Codwig or Rundle have a full brain between you."

"Watch your insults, Your Highness, or you will be eating this blade."

She sighed, but closed her mouth. That particular blade was not as friendly as a dull one would have been. Her arm had begun to sting quite painfully. After a few minutes of silence, she asked, "Where are we going?"

"Back to your beloved."

"What do you mean?"

The shorter man, Codwig, hit the taller one in the back of the head. "Not her beloved—her betrothed. We're taking ye to your betrothed, Prince Cylrick, to see how much he'll pay for ye."

"What are you implying? Do you honestly think I am some princess, and I am betrothed?" She started to chuckle. "You are having a laugh."

"Doesn't matter if you are or aren't. You still fit the description. We're still taking ye to him, and he'll still give us money."

"I am not betrothed to a prince!" she shouted as forcefully as possible to make them see she was not afraid.

"Then if you're not betrothed, I guess'n that means I can have ye for myself, eh?" the bigger man said, his beard wiggling when he talked.

"You're a pretty thing, and worth a pretty penny, too. Now tell me, Princess Kyra of Dillany, since I can see it in your eyes that you're afraid of us—though you be brave enough to pretend not to be. You be lyin' along with the rest of us. Now tell me, how much will your prince give you once we gets to his kingdom? Or do we just take ye ourselves and bring you back to our house?"

Then a strong voice declared behind them, "I will grant you whatever price you ask, as long as she is brought back to me unharmed."

CHAPTER SIXTEEN:

David could hear their bantering once he got close enough, and then simply swung around and followed behind them. His first impulse was to pounce on Marie and run off with her, but then he noticed she was nursing her arm. His next choice was to face the men head-on and hope for the best.

They looked him over from top to bottom, each man poised as if ready for a fight. "Who are ye?" the one with a beard asked. "You don't look like the prince we been meaning to do business with."

"I am Prince David. You are on my property and have stolen my guest. Now, unhand her at once, and I will see that you are both properly rewarded."

The shorter man looked from Marie to David and then back to Marie again. "My, my. She does know you. Look at her face. And now I have to wonder if she got herself caught up with two princes, or if she is really who she says she is."

"And who is that?" David asked.

"She says she's nobody."

"No!" The one with the beard started to laugh. "She was saying as how she was the prince's guard." He nearly doubled over in hysterics, the shorter man joining him.

Marie yanked the reins out of the taller man's hands and whipped the horse around, heading straight for David. "Come on!" she yelled.

David whipped his horse around and followed after her. "We're not going to get far!" he shouted. He could already hear the men chasing them as they broke through the forest into the road.

"I do not care. I want out of here, and I want out of here now!"

There was a distinct gunshot before Marie's horse crumpled below her. And then another bang, and David's expired to the same fate. Both of them tumbled into the road, the large beasts writhing around in pain. It was as David was attempting to get up that an immense hoof hit his head. He heard Marie's screams, and then all went black.

* * *

"Get up, dear."

David groaned as a distinctly female voice rang through his head.

"You have suffered a nasty fall and a very mean bump, but you are moving now, so I think it means you will be better. At least, I hope so."

He groaned again.

"Shh … Very well. Do not open your eyes, then. Perhaps it is best to sleep a little longer. I will be right here when you awaken."

Her voice sounded vaguely familiar. Young, cultured—pretty, even. Could a voice sound pretty? He smiled at the thought and then winced as his whole head exploded in pain.

When David came to again, he managed to peek one eye open. It was dark, and he could distinguish the faint smell of smoke. He opened his mouth to speak, but it was too dry to make a sound. There was a slight rustling beside him, and then that voice again.

"Prince David, are you awake?" she whispered next to him. "How are you feeling, dear?"

She had called him "dear" again. Whoever it was, she had the most charming voice. He reached over and clutched the top of her arm. Though he could not see her face, he was surprised at how close she was. Without another thought, he wrapped his other arm around her.

"David?" she gasped quietly.

Good heavens. It was Miss Marie. She was here and safely next to him. And then he brought her lips to his, not caring if he had enough to drink or not. There was nothing more that he wanted to taste right at that moment. She was stiff and frozen for a second, but then she relaxed and returned the kiss. Her sweet, soft hair framed his face as she melted into him. When she eventually lifted her head, all he wanted was to succumb to her honeyed lips again.

CHAPTER SEVENTEEN:

"Dearest," she whispered, "are you thirsty? Your lips are so parched, I fear you must be dreadfully so."

"Yes." There. He was able to speak.

She quickly left and then returned with a jug of water. Ever so slowly, he attempted to rise up upon his elbows while she held the cool liquid to his lips. Mmm. It was heaven. An angel and glorious water. What more could a man ask for?

"Would you like more?" she asked.

"Yes."

In less than a minute, Marie had returned and poured more vital water in his mouth.

"Thank you," he said as he clearly looked at her for the first time.

Miss Marie smiled back at him, the moonlight caressing her dark hair as it tumbled about her shoulders. "Hello."

"Hello," he responded, his eyes never leaving hers.

"You kissed me." She grinned, but did not move an inch closer.

"Aye, and you kissed me in return."

"What will my betrothed say about that?"

David attempted a shrug, but his shoulders could not do it. "I think he will say, 'It looks like you and I are not betrothed anymore.'"

"Do you think so?"

"Definitely."

She glanced away and grinned. "And what if he meets me and wishes to remain betrothed?"

"Then I will have to remind him that that is not possible because you are betrothed to me."

"Am I?"

"I kissed you."

"Yes." She bit her lip. "And that does usually mean a promise of sorts."

"Yes, it does. Especially with royalty."

"Does it? Especially with them?"

"Yes."

She stared at him for a long moment, and while she did so, he remembered the name of the princess the two men were certain she was. "Kyra?"

"Yes?"

He blinked, and then moved a bit closer to her. "Is your name truly Princess Kyra?"

"I . . . yes. It is me they are after."

"I am lying here, not wishing to ask what happened or where we are because I am afraid of ruining this moment. Instead, I shall stay here and admire you. I find myself completely captivated by the most beautiful and charming princess I have ever known."

"Oh, bosh!" She shook her head and then impulsively laid her cheek upon his chest. "I will not ruin this moment either to tell you the horrid position we are both in. Instead, I will enjoy these stolen minutes a bit longer while the despicable monsters have drunken themselves into a sleep-filled stupor."

He choked on a lungful of air. "They are drunk and asleep this very moment?" He attempted to get up, but she would not move.

"'Tis no use—neither of us are going anywhere. We cannot escape. I have thought of all possible ways of leaving while you have slept, and I tell you for a certainty, it would take a miracle."

"Surely not. I cannot be in that bad of shape, and you clearly have your wits about you. I am positive that together, we could make it back to the castle before either of them are the wiser."

She grinned, leaned over, and kissed him again.

"On second thought, why not enjoy a small coze for a bit?" David returned the kiss. He did not know if the moon had moved that small fraction, or perhaps a cloud had slid away, but whatever had happened in that moment, he noticed the pain on her features. "What is wrong?" His heart clenched in sympathy for what she was struggling to hide from him. "You are in pain, my dearest. Something is wrong. Tell me."

She shook her head. "Nay, all is well. You sleep and get your head healed, and perhaps tomorrow, we shall talk about me and the silly trouble that I am."

"Princess Kyra? Good heavens, there is so much I wish to know about you right now. So very many questions I have, but first, please ease my heart a bit and tell me you are fine. That they have done nothing to you."

She attempted a laugh. "No. They have done nothing. I doubt they will ever wish to touch me again. I doubt anyone will."

Right at that moment, he caught the tiniest glimmer in the corner of her eye. "What happened to you? I remember that a horse's hoof found my head. I saw you fall—are you well?" He could not see past her beautiful face to tell if anything else was amiss. "What is it? Will you not be brave enough to share with me?"

She took a deep breath and grinned. "No. You need rest. Tomorrow will be time enough to share with you all that I can. For tonight, let's let the sleeping prince be, and hopefully you will think this all was just a dream."

"The part about being betrothed to you? Is that what you speak of?"

"That and more." She kissed him again.

"The kisses too? You are hoping I forget all this?" He wrapped his arm around her waist. "I must warn you now, dearest. I am fully awake and quite capable of remembering every moment with you lying upon my chest in such a way."

"Oh!" She quickly pulled back. "How brazen of me! Forgive me."

David chuckled at those sweet lips in such shock. She truly was the most adorable creature he had ever known. And she was indeed a princess as well! Oh, how wonderfully the world aligned at times. "I will not tell, if you do not."

If the sun had been shining, he was certain he would see her blush. As it was, he could hardly see past her face to whatever was bothering her. David turned over so he could sit up more fully and ascertain what had happened to her, but she put her hand to his shoulder.

"Please, give me one more night of dignity. I beg of you, allow me to dream of this amazing moment with you because I fear it will all be gone in the morning."

"Whatever in the world are you talking about?"

"David." It was her eyes, imploring him to respect this wish, that were his undoing.

As curious and worried and distraught as he was, the princess was obviously in much more distress than he first imagined her to be. "If you need help, we must act immediately."

"Shh …" She closed her eyes and then smiled again. "All is well. For tonight, everything is well."

How could he deny her this? There was a point in every fragile relationship where one must allow the other respect and trust they knew what was best. He lay back down on the hard ground and held out his arms. "Only if you promise to keep my chest company some more, for I assure you, I have never experienced a more wonderful feeling than that of you so close to me."

Without hesitation, the hidden princess lay back down with a smile. After several minutes of slowly trailing his hand through her hair, he began to hear the sweet sound of her even breathing, indicating she had finally fallen asleep. Then, with the angel in his arms, he spent the rest of the evening with his mind racing in deep concern for her and their predicament. Who was the enchanting Princess Kyra, and why were such men after her? His mind twisted and turned over this question, determined to make sense of what he could not fathom. What else was she not telling him? Everything about the glorious creature was shrouded in mystery, but one thing was for certain—his heart had come too far to turn back now. He would defend her and protect her until his last breath. No matter what the outcome, David vowed in the wee hours of the morning to love her forever.

CHAPTER EIGHTEEN:

David woke up to the sound of shouting, and in his disoriented state, he attempted to get up before he thought better of it. Instantly, he became woozy, and his head began to throb. However, he managed to pull himself up from the ground, using a large boulder near him for leverage.

He was outside near a campfire, and his aching body reminded him that he had slept on the hard ground all night long. The shouts were not helping his headache at all. He turned to see what the commotion was and then stopped. All of a sudden, the words that were being yelled were understood.

"No one will want you now, you useless piece of baggage!" one of the men declared as he looked down in disgust. "What are we to do with that?" He pointed at a very solemn Marie—nay, Kyra—with her head in her hands sitting below the two men on the dirt.

"Fat chance that prince of yours will not run away screaming once he seen the likes of you!" the other man exclaimed. "How are we to get our reward money now?"

"You are a despicable tart and should be left here on the roadside, where you will most likely be begging for food the rest of ye days!" The man kicked her with his boot, and Kyra yelped in pain.

Anger flashed through David. "What is the meaning of this?" He stood up as tall as he could and took two steps toward them. "Do not dare touch her again!"

"Oh, look! Her other little prince is awake," the bigger man sneered. "Though I guarantee, he will not be so loyal once he sees you!"

"Come here!" the shorter one taunted. "Come and see the mess the princess has made of herself. And sees if we want anything to do with her, because we don't! We're done with the both of you. I suggest you leave her where she's at and get on home and tell your mama and papa all about the big, bad men who hurt you."

The other one cackled. "Of course, we'll be long gone before anyone finds us." He headed over to the campfire and began to gather up his things. "All of this for nothing. For a stupid girl who isn't worth a hill of beans!"

The shorter man began to pack up too. "The ugly thing deserves to die for what pains she's caused us. Getting rolled over by that horse!"

"You are the apes who shot the horse!" Kyra looked up to shout at them.

"Shut your vile trap! We've had enough from ye today."

"Don't talk to her that way!" David felt as though he were walking through thick molasses as he slowly made his way to the princess.

"Gladly!" one of the men replied as he jumped upon his horse. "We'll let you do it for us."

The other was still laughing. "Aye, he being doing that and much worse in a minute." They rode off, and in a moment, the whole place became peacefully still.

"Forgive me for not having my wits about me enough to preserve your honor," David said as he gingerly sat down next to her.

Kyra's hair covered her features as she kept her face averted from him.

"Are you well? You will not let their words reach you, my dear. You are much better than whatever their anger can produce."

She nodded her head and then sniffed.

He had never been good with weeping females, but he had to try something. "When his boot struck you, did it hurt?"

"Yes."

"Was it your leg?"

"Yes."

"Come here. Let me see how to fix it for you."

"No." Her eyes whipped to his, and her hands clutched her skirts. "Please do not look under there."

David sat back and then stammered, "For—forgive me. I was not implying to lift up your skirts, but merely to check to see if something was broken."

It was then that he noticed the dark circles under her eyes and the faded look deep within their depths. She was clearly in tremendous pain. In an instant, he wanted to kick himself for not insisting they left last night. "Dearest, how can I help you?"

She closed her eyes and ducked her head toward the ground before saying softly, "Everything hurts so much, I doubt there is anything you can do. I will most likely be this way forever."

"What hurts?"

"My back, arms, and chest. And my legs should more than likely hurt a great deal more than they do."

"From when he kicked you?"

She shook her head. "No. From the horse."

"What are you saying, Kyra?"

"I am saying, I cannot walk, and I doubt I will ever be able to walk again."

This time, David did not ask for permission. He lifted her skirts to her knees and then gasped. Great heavens. How was she even speaking to him? How was she conscious? Her legs were so mangled and indeed broken, he could not fathom how she could bear such pain.

"Just leave me, please. Those men were right. No one will ever want me now."

"You need medical attention immediately." He felt as though he were about to be sick. "I cannot believe you did not tell me of this. I have been lying around like a dolt, not even thinking of this misery you must be in."

"David, hush. It is not all that bad. I cannot feel much of my legs at the moment. Though do not accidentally bump me with your foot, because that seems to send sharp pains from my leg all the way up my back."

At that moment, he understood how horrid her life had become. The sweet, happy princess of the pea field was now utterly crippled. And she was correct. No one would ever want her now. Not even his own family.

CHAPTER NINETEEN:

Kyra gasped as Prince David lifted her up into his arms and then stood up. Pain shot through her whole frame. "What are you doing? Put me down at once!"

"I am taking you home. Well, not your home. Mine. And hopefully, we can get you help and be sure your parents are contacted as well."

"My parents? I wrote them a letter. I am certain they are already on their way here."

"Yes. However, it is probably best if we got you to the castle."

He bounced her slightly as he began to walk back the way they came. Kyra winced, but could not believe he was attempting it. Surely it was too far to carry her. The prince would most likely become excessively tired or injured.

"What about your head? You cannot mean to carry me the whole way."

"I intend to do just that. Now avert your eyes, for we will be coming upon the horses soon, and I do not wish to distress you more."

"I am much more concerned with you carrying me than the sight of dead horses." Which was not perfectly true. Seeing Thunder lying upon the ground would not help her. She tucked her head into the hollow of David's throat. Perhaps it was best if she attempted to distract them both. "Yes, well, odd how it is once you come face to face with your abductors, you suddenly feel you can trust those you were once worried about."

"Did I frighten you before?"

"Oh, most definitely. Especially when your guards brought my other carriage horse to the castle. I did not know if your family was behind my overturned coach, if your kingdom was my enemy, or if you happened upon my horse all on your own. I did not know who I could trust, and I was completely lost."

"So it was your carriage my guards found mangled."

"Yes, and I have no idea where my servants have gone. Or if they are alive. I have heard nothing."

"My family was concerned you might have been hiding, and had something to do with the attack."

"Are you implying they thought I was one of the bandits?"

He shrugged. "You refused to tell us the truth of who you were. It was a secret, and until everything was solved, my parents, especially, were leery of you."

If everything was not so awful right now, she would probably laugh. "How did they know I was not telling the truth?"

"I believe my mother noticed the fabric of your gown and announced quite decidedly that you were royalty. So she sent us to work in the pea fields to prove it."

"What? You mean you usually do not go out there?"

"Ha. No. Not if I can help it. Though, I do have to say, you had me fooled with how easily you adjusted out there, making a game of everything and causing us all to laugh. You certainly seemed like a commoner then. A very enjoyable commoner, or so I told my mother."

He continued as he walked out onto the main road. "She still was not convinced, and it gave me hope. I find the more I have been with you, the more I have grown to enjoy myself. You are exceedingly fun and energetic and brave." He took a deep breath and then said near her ear, "And now, Princess Kyra, I hope you can let your guard down a bit and know that you are safe now. We will do everything in our power to see that you make it home without any more mishaps."

"The bandits are still loose."

"Which is precisely why the second we make it home, I will have my men search the kingdom over."

He began to walk very quickly, and Kyra made sure her eyes were closed, since he was most likely walking past Thunder and his horse.

David's voice rose. "We need to find out why they targeted you, and what more they wanted other than ransom. We still need to locate your servants and find out who was behind this. Someone knew your likeness. Someone set them up to this. Bandits like that do not lie in wait for princesses who happen to be traveling through without some sort of tipoff. Someone told them you were coming to meet your betrothed and when you would be on the roads and what your carriage looked like. That person will be found as well."

From the conviction in his voice and his strong shoulders, she felt very safe, as if she could trust anything he said.

"Prince David!" came a shout from behind them— toward the lake.

He turned to look over his shoulder, and they both let out a sigh of relief when they saw his guards on their horses coming toward them.

"Ho!" he hailed the closest. "Help me with Princess Kyra of Dillany. Her legs have been damaged, and she cannot walk."

"Yes, Your Highness." The man jumped down and gently collected Kyra from him. "We will get the best doctors in the land to help you."

"Thank you," she responded a bit shyly. She did not think she would ever get used to being carried by a man.

"Can you sit upon a horse, Your Highness, or shall I send for a carriage?" the guard asked.

David was walking toward another guard when he turned around and addressed the man carrying her. "Go and get the carriage. She would not be comfortable jarring in the seat of a saddle. She is in a great deal of pain. I am going to relay everything I know to Captain Davis, and then will be back to retrieve her from you."

Kyra shook her head. "Please do not overly trouble yourselves."

"Nonsense. We will see that you are as comfortable as possible." David then headed toward the captain. "How did you find us?"

"When you did not return last night, the queen sent us out to search for you early this morning. We have been around this whole countryside and lake searching, only to find you walking on the road, no less. What happened to Miss—er, the princess?"

Kyra interrupted them. "The horse I rode was shot, and I was crushed beneath it as it writhed in agony." She nodded her head toward David. "I believe Prince David is also in great pain."

The captain's eyebrows went up, and he immediately called two of his soldiers forward. "You, run to the castle—make haste, do as the prince has ordered, and bring back a carriage," he said to one man and then glanced at the other. "You, go toward the south and find the king. Let him know the search is off and the prince is alive. Then meet us at the castle."

"Yes, sir." The soldiers bowed in their saddles and then raced away on their steeds.

"The queen will be so relieved to know you are here."

The two men spoke in hushed tones for a few minutes and then David asked, "Any news of Princess Kyra's parents?"

"None. I will send another guard immediately to them."

It would be so wonderful to head back home at last. It was directly to the west, a two-day drive by carriage, if they stopped overnight.

"You." David pointed to a young man. "Go. Race like the wind and bring her family to the castle. Let them know as much as you can, and tell them that their daughter is being looked after as well as possible. I will take her back now."

"You are too kind," Kyra said as he gently removed her from the guard's arms.

David shook his head and then walked over to the side of the road. Another guard quickly removed a saddle blanket and set it on the ground for them. David gingerly sat down with her and then said, "No, we are doing our duty." Those green eyes met hers, and her heart flip-flopped inside her chest. "I would never forgive myself if you were not safe." Then his lips met hers once more in a tender kiss as they were sitting upon the roadside where anyone could see.

CHAPTER TWENTY:

Ironically, the carriage arrived just as Kyra's parents and traveling guards made their way up the road. "That's my father!" Kyra cried out. She was still nestled in David's arms sitting along the roadside. "Quick, flag them down. He must have left as soon as they received my letter."

A guard stepped into the road and waved his arms for them to halt. They cautiously waited several yards away as a Dillany guard came forward on his horse.

"Yes?" the uniformed man asked.

David hugged her and spoke loudly. "We have Princess Kyra here."

"Tell my mother and father that I must speak with them immediately," she added.

The guard did not hesitate and rode off.

"Now, how do we explain this?" David whispered in her ear. "They are expecting to find their daughter at my castle. Even though you tried to escape from there, it is where they are expecting to find you."

"I know, I know." She shook her head. "If I had not attempted to head home . . . Never mind. They are coming."

A large carriage pulled up, and a tall, finely dressed man and woman climbed out. "What is the meaning of this?" Her father walked forward and looked shocked at seeing her in David's arms. "Kyra, remove yourself from his embrace at once!"

"You are here!" she said.

"Yes. And why are you *there*?" her mother asked. "And in broad daylight, no less." The older woman stood with her hands on her hips. "Indeed, we believed you were in grave danger and have rushed the whole way only to find you clinging to a man on the roadside!"

"She was in grave danger. Well, not when she was at my home, but she did not know it," David replied.

"And who are you?" her father asked.

"Prince David of Haltaen Court. I came and tried to rescue your daughter from some bandits."

Her mother looked perplexed and beckoned to Kyra. "Come here, daughter, and tell me what is going on." Kyra did not move. The queen glanced around at the guards and then whispered loudly, "Is he harming you? Your letter said—"

"What did your letter say?" David asked, looking down at her. "Did you imply that I had hurt you?"

Her father nearly lost his temper. "Is this why he continues to hold you against our wishes? Young man, release my daughter at once." Instantly, the guards behind the king and queen unsheathed their swords and pointed them directly at David.

"Wait!" Kyra sputtered.

David's guards pulled their swords out as well.

"Wait a moment!" David raised his hands, but it was not doing much good, with them both on the ground as they were and everyone else standing.

Kyra knew she had to be the one to speak. "I cannot move, Father. I believe I have been crippled. The bandits shot my horse as I attempted to flee. The horse crushed me. Prince David is merely holding me so I do not have to be upon the hard ground as we awaited the carriage. It has just been brought so I could arrive at the castle in comfort."

"Prince David is not your abductor?" her mother asked.

"No, though I thought he might be involved. I have since learned that he is a hero and came to save me. However, neither of us fared as well as we would have liked."

The queen spoke again. "And what do you mean, you are crippled? Is this why you are still in his arms?"

Kyra took a deep breath. "Yes, that is what I am trying to explain. I cannot move, and everything hurts so much. Oh, Mother, I am so happy to see you!"

"My dearest daughter." Her mother walked over to the pair of them and crumpled to her knees. "Oh, put those swords away, Henry! I have no idea what to make of this mess, yet I am certain we will be able to sort it all out later. Can you not see our poor daughter has been injured?" She then looked to Kyra. "My dear, can you truly not move your legs at all?"

Kyra shook her head.

"Are you in pain?"

And then the first of Kyra's tears broke. She had held on for as long as she possibly could, but seeing her mother finally, it could not be helped. "Yes. 'Tis what frightens me most. Indeed, though I am in agony, I should be in so much more pain than I am."

"May I?" The queen leaned over and raised Kyra's skirts a bit—as privately as possible—to examine her twisted legs. And then she gasped. "Henry, she needs medical attention immediately."

David tightened his hold. "There should be a doctor waiting at the castle now for her."

"How far away is that?"

"A few miles up the road," David answered.

Her mother and father shared a concerned look.

"How bad is it?" Henry asked.

Her mother met his gaze. "Very bad."

He took a deep breath and then looked at his guards. "Put your swords away, men. These people are not our enemies." Then he moved toward Kyra and crouched down with his arms out. "Will you please allow me to carry her?"

"Of course."

David released his hold, and Kyra felt herself being held in her father's arms as if she were a little girl who had fallen asleep in the parlor again. He used to pick her up and carry her back to her room while she pretended to be asleep. It was oddly comforting to be held again.

"What will happen to me, Papa?"

He looked down into her eyes, and for the first time, she saw the fatigue and worry etching his brow. "I do not know, little one, but first let us be very, very grateful you are safe now."

"I am sorry I attempted to come home on my own. I never should have thought to do so. If not, I would have still been at David's castle, safe and sound."

He walked her over to the family's carriage and then climbed inside with her. "My daughter, I am deeply saddened to see you harmed. Your mother and I have been blaming ourselves for allowing you to go on this trip to begin with. However, one cannot look back. It is wise to learn from one's mistakes."

"Do you really believe so?"

"Henry?" Kyra's mother poked her head into the carriage.

"Yes, Patricia?"

"Prince David has asked if he could travel with us. What say you?"

"Does he not have his own carriage awaiting him?"

She glanced over her shoulder and then lowered her voice. "Yes, but he is anxious to be with Kyra."

"Are we not to have any time with our daughter now that we have found her?"

Patricia gave a shrug. "Apparently not."

He sighed and moved over to the side of the bench seat so that her mother could join them. "Tell the prince to come in, though why he cannot wait a few minutes, I will never know."

David's eyes met Kyra's as he climbed into the carriage. "Thank you for allowing me to travel with you, Your Majesties, Princess."

"You are most welcome." Kyra grinned as he sat across from them.

"I know I am making a cake of myself being so bold, but you must understand, I have been extremely worried about Princess Kyra for some time now. I would like to guarantee that nothing happens to her."

Kyra could feel her father's muscles tense in disapproval, but was grateful he did not say anything to contradict the young prince. He rapped upon the top of the coach and told the man to hurry them to the castle as soon as possible.

"Follow the guards, and you will come right to a large building," David called. "I let them know to head home. They should be leaving as we speak."

The coach jerked forward, and all three began the journey back to the castle.

CHAPTER TWENTY-ONE:

The castle was a flurry of motion as Kyra was whisked away and taken to her room upstairs. David's heart would not settle, and he refused all medical help for his head wound until he knew how Kyra would fare. He paced the hallways for nearly two hours, answering whatever questions he could from his parents, but mostly he attempted to calm his racing mind.

He was terrified for her, and the longer the doctor took, the more positive he was that the outcome would not be good. His head throbbed painfully and his legs and back ached, yet he ignored it all because the sweetest girl he had ever known was also one of the least complaining and the bravest. If she could face all she had without a murmur for herself, then why would he complain of his cuts and bruises? Good heavens, at least he could still walk.

David took a deep breath and slumped down on a small cushioned bench in the corridor nearest Kyra's room. His mother was soon to join him. She had one of the servants bring up a pot of tea and move a table near them as well.

"Here," she said as she passed him a steaming cup. "It will give your hands something to do."

"Thank you." David took the warm cup and saucer and sipped.

His mother did the same. The two sat in silence for a few minutes.

"What if she has lost the use of her legs?" he asked.

She sighed and shook her head. "The poor dear girl. I cannot imagine such a fate. But you can be sure that your father and his men will do everything in our power to see that these ruffians who did this to her will be brought to justice."

"Why would they even attempt such a thing? How could they possibly believe they could get away with something so cruel?"

"To think she was the hidden princess all along. And it was her carriage that had been vandalized."

"Have you heard any word of the servants who accompanied her?"

"Nay. Not a one," she responded. "Though there has been another body recovered at the site of the accident. Looked as though the man walked several feet before falling into a bush of some sort and died."

"One of her servants?"

"We do not believe so. It looks to be another bandit. He was shot at close range with a pistol that the coachman most likely carried with him."

"Serves him right."

She nodded. "No one should go about overturning coaches and frightening princesses."

David turned more toward her. "It must have been one of her servants who led them to her in the first place."

"Your father and I think the same. Or a pub or innkeeper, if they had stops along their way."

"Right." He took a deep breath. "I had not thought of others who had met her by chance. They were attempting to hold her for ransom money, wanting her betrothed to pay for her."

"So you have said." She stood up as if she were agitated. "But why? This is what I cannot understand. Something is most definitely not right here. There would be no reason for them to put themselves into such danger for the girl. None. They had to have known she would be protected and that they would be found. And why would her betrothed pay for her? Why not send the ransom demand to her parents instead?"

"There is so much I do not understand either. Chiefly being, why did they let me go free? I am a prince and worth just as much as she, and yet they did not attempt to coerce you or Father out of money. As soon as they saw that Princess Kyra was damaged, they bolted. It was such an odd reaction."

"Yes, but thankfully, they did leave. Especially with how damaged you both are." She touched his head. "Truly, David, you should have someone look at this."

He gently brushed her hand away. "It is nothing. Right now, my worry is for the princess alone. I will heal, but she may not."

Concern marred his mother's features. "David, what if she *is* crippled?"

"What do you mean?"

She glanced down the long corridor and then back at him. "How could we bear the sight of her, disfigured as she is?"

His jaw dropped. Though he knew his mother would react this way, it still pained him to hear her speak such nonsense. However, he gave her the benefit of the doubt and said, "It will be difficult, I am sure. The poor thing. I am hoping to do whatever I can for her."

She looked at him sharply. "What do you mean by that statement? Surely you are not implying your feelings have continued to develop for the girl, are you?"

He shrugged and then gave a small grin. "Would it matter overly much if I did?"

"David!" She gasped and sat back down. "I have no problem being hospitable to strangers and helping them in their time of need, but one must know when to set boundaries and look forward to the stranger's departure."

"That is the most ridiculous thing I have ever heard you say. Be kind, care for people, yet be grateful when they scurry away?"

"This is your life we are talking about, my son! This is not a lark or game to find yourself bewitched by someone who is wholly unsuited for you."

"In which way is she unsuited for me? Kyra is a princess, and therefore she is on—"

"No." She folded her arms. "You have a duty to fulfill for your country. I told you from the beginning not to grow attached to her, and now more than ever, it would seem those words have proven extremely wise."

"And why is that, Mother?" he asked, daring her to say the words she was thinking.

His mother must have realized she was being taunted, for in the next moment, her eyes flashed and she declared, "My son will never attach himself to a cripple. He needs someone who will stand by his side and run this kingdom as she ought."

There was the distinct sound of someone clearing their throat, and they turned to find King Henry standing in the hall.

CHAPTER TWENTY-TWO:

King Henry looked at them both and said, "Our worst fears have been realized. My dearest daughter has been crippled." He lifted his chin a notch. "Due to the conversation I had the most unfortunate privilege to overhear just now, we will not be trespassing here much longer."

David's mother was all flustered apologies. "I beg your pardon. It was extremely rude to imply that you are not welcome here, for you are all welcome as long as it is needed. Traveling with such an invalid may be quite out of the question at the moment."

He raised his chin a fraction higher. "Pardon me, but it would not be as painful as overhearing what I have just been privy to." He bowed low. "Excuse me. I merely came here to inform you of the doctor's verdict, as you so generously requested. Now I must speak with my wife. We will be leaving within the hour."

"King Henry, please stay!" His mother stood and took a few steps after the man who had spun on his heel and was even then striding back into Kyra's room.

The door shut with a resounding click.

David's stomach suddenly began to churn. "Well, that was uncomfortable."

His mother wrapped an arm around her middle and paced. "I cannot believe that just happened. How long had he been standing there? What did he hear?"

"He heard enough to be extremely offended."

She nodded, her lips forming a frown. "I have never been ashamed of anything more in my life. I feel incredibly dreadful."

"You never should have said those words about the princess." David felt a flash of anger course through him. "She is a girl whose life will never be the same. A cheerful, happy, intelligent being who now has the life of an invalid because of the actions of another. She deserves only our love and friendship, not our censure."

"David!" She closed her eyes a moment. "How could you say such a thing? I was not censuring the poor girl. I was only pointing out that she would not make a suitable wife for you."

His gaze connected with hers. "And that is enough. Just the tone of your voice. Your implications are great indeed. And now you have guaranteed that I shall never get close enough to her even to be a friend."

"Of all the gibberish. Of course you can be a friend! Son, you are becoming more and more dramatic by the second. This was just a little mishap, and I will be able to clear it all up as soon as I have a moment to explain our exchange a little better."

And still, he would not be appeased by her easy dismissal. "Explain what, Mother? That you believe I am greater than their daughter? That she is not worthy of love? What? Just precisely how were you planning on correcting this blunder?"

She threw her hands up and began to walk back down the corridor. "Very well. You are determined to see me as the enemy—perhaps I am. I do not know why I bother to speak with you at all." With that, she started to head down the stairs.

David could hear the echo of her voice as she began to instruct the servants to prepare for the imminent departure of Princess Kyra and her family.

He walked back over to his bench and sat down again. His eyes never strayed from Kyra's door. Just like that, she would be gone, long before he had the opportunity to really get to know her. And her whole world would forever be changed because of what happened on his land.

His world would forever be changed because of what happened on his land. It was as if he was about to miss out on an opportunity. And did he blame her father for reacting as he did? Of course not. Why would they stay?

In that one fateful moment, their kingdom's reputation for generous hospitality had dissolved. And what could he do about it? Nothing. Absolutely nothing.

He leaned back on the bench and let out a sigh of disgust. The worst thing was, he could imagine that King Henry had just blurted out the rudeness to his wife, with Kyra no doubt in earshot. She would know what the queen thought of her before he had a chance to explain that not everyone in the castle felt the same way.

David had to do something. He could not sit here like a coward and hope to make amends as Kyra's family left the castle. Something must be done now. He abruptly walked over and knocked upon the door without having an inkling of what to say.

A moment later, the door swung open. King Henry looked down his nose at him. "Yes?" he inquired.

David could see Kyra sitting up in a makeshift bed in the middle of the room. It looked like her family had removed a few of the mattresses and placed them in the center of the floor, probably so the doctor could have easier access to her legs. Kyra's eyes were red and swollen, as well as her mother's. The queen was on a chair near her bedside, clutching Kyra's hands, and both were looking at him expectantly. He cleared his throat. "I—I hope my mother's words did not harm you during this difficult time."

Kyra tilted her head. "What are you speaking of?"

David's gaze flew to her father's, and that man gave a short shake of his head as if to say, "Do not speak of this to her. She has no idea."

Did the king not say a word to her, then? David went to take a step into the room, and the king blocked him. "Why are you here?"

David glanced once more at Kyra and then whispered, "I did not say those things. My mother did."

"I am well aware of your stance. I heard it all, but I am not prepared for you to be in a room with my daughter in her bed."

David flushed and stepped back. "I beg your pardon! I had not thought . . . I did not mean to imply . . ."

"Henry, what are you saying to the young prince? Let him in," the queen called. "Kyra is very desirous to speak to him."

"Not in her chamber. It is not done. You know this, Patricia."

She laughed and made a small motion with her hand. "Goodness. We are right here. There is no need for such ceremony when you know perfectly well our daughter cannot be anywhere else at the moment." The queen waved him forward. "Come here, young man. Come and lift our spirits, for as you can see, this has been a very difficult day for all of us."

He took one more glance at her disapproving father and then stepped around him and into the room. There was no way he would miss an opportunity to be with her. "Is it true? Are you crippled?"

CHAPTER TWENTY-THREE:

Kyra looked into David's worried eyes and attempted to put on a brave face, though it felt as if a part of her had died. "The doctor says that I will most likely be unable to walk again. But there are special chairs on wheels that my parents are going to look into for me, where I can be pushed around. Is that not grand?"

"What will become of you?"

Her face fell. Could he not see that she was desperately trying to stay cheerful? "I suppose I will be the same person I have always been, but without legs, of course."

"Without them?" He flinched. "Will the doctor amputate?"

That was the worst of all the news she had been made to bear. "He is saying they are too mangled to be saved. If the doctor does not cut them off, an infection will grow, and I will die."

Queen Patricia squeezed Kyra's hand and then gave a forced laugh. "Let us speak of more pleasant things, like perhaps the weather, or . . . or, goodness, I do not know. My mind is all in shambles at the moment, but I am certain there is something else we could discuss. Is there not?"

Kyra watched David close his eyes and then chew on his bottom lip before looking determinedly at them both. "I do not know if this is a better subject, but I vow to you all that I will catch the villains who have done this. I will personally see to it that they get their dues."

"And will you find our servants for us too?" Kyra asked. "I have been so worried about them. Since neither my father nor mother have heard from them, we fear the worst."

"Come now, dear," her mother interrupted. "We are thinking happy thoughts now."

King Henry walked over to the bed and sat upon a chair near the foot of it. "Young man, once I remove the queen and my daughter from here and transport them home, I would like to join you on your quest to find these bandits. I have a score to settle with them as well."

"I would gladly accept any and all help I can get." David stood a bit straighter. "In fact, I shall inform the other kingdoms and see if we cannot recruit others as well to help."

"Very good," her father replied. "We certainly do not want other monarchies to experience this. Those men are vile and should be punished."

"Father," Kyra blurted, "who do you think is behind this?"

He shook his head. "I do not know, but we do not need to have such vileness here. For years, we have been peaceful kingdoms, coexisting amicably. I would like to see that it stays that way. Even if there is a disturbance targeting our land, our family, we will get to the bottom of it and attempt to smooth everything to how it was before."

"Do you have any enemies?" David asked. "Do you know of anyone who would wish you harm?"

"Not that I know of," her father said, "though I do not doubt there are some who must become irritated from time to time. Yet why target and harm my daughter, I will never understand."

"Wait a moment." Kyra looked between the two men. "Why must it be someone attacking us? Was it not Prince Cylrick they were hoping to extract money from? Could it possibly be his kingdom they are targeting, and I was merely a pawn?"

"Perhaps, though with how quickly they snatched up Prince David, they would have been using him for ransom as well," her mother said.

"'Tis true!" David looked surprised.

"I did not think of that," Kyra said. She took a deep breath and then rubbed her forehead. "All of it is too confusing. And it does not make sense to me that they would leave so easily." She looked down at her legs covered by the ornate quilt. "Unless I truly am worthless now—then the irony of this situation has not been lost on me. They wanted me, they hurt me, and then they let me go. Kind of humorous, is it not?" She said it, though she did feel extremely small and hopeless.

"No. It is not humorous at all!" Her mother stood up. "Do not fret because you have lost your legs. Look at life as if it were a new adventure. We all shall. And we will overcome this, I promise."

Kyra smiled. How she loved her mother. How she loved every bit of bravery and gumption she was presenting at the moment. And how she needed a champion on her side.

"I am with the queen, Princess Kyra. Even though I did not have long to get to know you, you brought life into this castle I have never seen before. Indeed, your personality, your kindness, your easy way of seeing the good around you—you have changed me. I fear I do not know what will happen when you are gone."

Kyra blushed and then laughed. For the first time in hours, she truly laughed. "David, you act as though I am withering away and dying."

"Well, you could be doing just that, for all I know. How am I to distinguish otherwise?"

"Are you asking to continue to stay in correspondence with me?" she asked, her heart beginning to pick up speed. "Even after you have captured the bandits, you would still like to write to me?"

"Of course. I would love to. Write, visit, laugh …"

Her mother put her hand upon his arm. "Prince David, choose your words very carefully right now, for I fear it would seem as if you are asking earnestly to court my daughter."

David blinked and then looked at Kyra as if he were seeing her for the very first time.

It was such an odd stare, she attempted to brush it off. "Clearly he did not mean that, Mother. He is merely asking that we remain friends."

"No." David then glanced at her father. "No, I am in earnest. You are correct, Your Majesty. I would most sincerely wish to court your daughter. Though I did not think it was possible, as she is betrothed to another."

"You would wish to court her, even as disfigured as she is?" Her father spoke deliberately. "And even though she is promised, as you say?"

"If I have your permission, then yes. I would desire that more than anything. I fear—though she does not know it—that I have already lost my heart to her."

Kyra gasped. "David?"

He did not quite meet her gaze. "I will need some time to prove myself to her. To get to know her and hopefully truly court her."

Her father fidgeted in his seat. "And you will have no objections from your family over such a suit?"

The prince and Henry shared a look, and then finally David said, "Does it matter? I would follow my heart in this instance. And I believe you would wish for her to be protected and loved by someone who was willing to do just that."

Kyra did not know whether to cry in disbelief or sing in joy. However, she did understand one thing. "David, please do not do this to yourself. Please consider your duty to your family. I am not that wonderful, and you should wish for a whole queen to stand by your side."

"No." He remained firm. "You do not know me if you believe such drivel. I wish to have a queen I can speak to, turn to for advice, and mostly, laugh with and love. You do not have to have legs to do this. You are perfect just as you are."

CHAPTER TWENTY-FOUR:

King Henry stood and walked over to David. "Young man, though your words are strong and honorable, I fear I will need to see some dedication first. You would be taking on a larger task than you realize. You must see something of the world, to look at other women to court. Then, if your heart is still beating for my beautiful Princess Kyra, come find her and court her."

"Are you jesting?" David asked, his heart suddenly cold.

"No, I am being perfectly serious. I cannot have someone say one thing and then a few years later, decide it is all too difficult and break her heart when you choose to leave her and find love elsewhere. She is too precious for such a life."

"I agree."

"Then I wish you the best." The king took a deep breath and looked over at his daughter. "You may write one another, but I would ask that Prince David wait two years before he began a court with you, my dear. After that time, if he earnestly wishes to be with you still, then by all means, I will grant my blessing."

"Two years is an eternity!" David was beyond frustrated.

"Not if you are sincere."

"Please, Father, would you not reconsider?" Kyra asked.

David glanced over at her stricken face and knew she did not believe he would come back to her in two years' time. Perhaps her father was wise after all, for when David returned, she would truly know that he loved her and would not believe he had wed her out of pity. Yet he worried if she could get through those years without him—they would be extremely difficult.

Kyra's handsome prince took another step toward the bed and then looked directly at her as if they were the only two within the room. He knelt down and collected one of her hands into both of his. After kissing the top and sending the most wondrous of shivers down her spine, he began to speak.

"Princess Kyra, I do not know what will happen to each of us in the next two years. I am not a wizard, and I do not profess to know the future. However, I wish you to understand something. My dearest, you are looking at a man who would do anything for you. Anything. And it pains me greatly to imagine the next years without seeing your smile again, or hearing your laughter. Yet, my dear, though my heart will surely miss you, it will remain steadily beating only for you."

He took a deep breath and then continued, "You will doubt my heart many times. You will be upset, and your spirits will fall again and again as the realization of your condition continues to manifest itself in new hardships. Kyra, in those moments of doubt and feelings of despair or selflessness, please, my dearest, I implore you to remember this moment. Remember that a man loved you despite what you may fear most. Remember that it is not your outer shell that makes a person, but your soul—your smile, your laughter, your words, and yes, even your frustrations, fears, and anger—all lead me directly to you."

She could not imagine such words from anyone. It was as if he was speaking to her heart the exact things it needed to hear—things she had no idea she needed to hear until that moment.

"I will continue to hunt for the men who did this. I will search for them valiantly until they are all captured and this mystery is solved. Yet I know it is not that feat that will cheer you in the long days when we are apart, and I daresay it will be lonely and disheartening for me, knowing I cannot come to you and be there for you when things get rough. I could slay a thousand bandits—nay, a thousand dragons—and that would still not give you the comfort of knowing you are worth more than a pair of legs.

"And so, I kneel here as a reminder that I will return. I will think of you steadily. I will prove to your family that I am worthy of you, and I will hold you again. All I need from you is an affirmation that you would wish my suit. If you said no, I would withdraw this offer, but the decision is yours."

She could not help herself. Without warning, two large tears began to fall upon her cheeks.

"No, sweetest. Do not cry. It is silly to cry at this time," he said.

"I know." She sniffed. "I could not imagine such words ever being said, whether I had legs or not. I do not believe I am worth waiting two years for. Those are by far the most incredible words ever spoken."

"Are they?" He began to smile. "Are they truly?"

She nodded. Oh, how she loved his smile.

"And what of Prince Cylrick?" he asked.

King Henry answered, "I will give him the same guidance. If he wishes to court Kyra, he will have to wait two years and see if his heart does not lead him elsewhere."

"And will he be permitted to write her letters as well?"

"Of course," the queen said.

"What if I prefer Prince David to him?" Kyra asked.

"Then it will be your choice." Her father sat back down into the chair. "Honestly, I was quite impressed with that speech, young man. I could not imagine anyone saying something as tenderly and as heartfelt to my daughter. Thank you for that."

Her mother smiled. "It was very touching. I can see that you are commendable, and I hope you will renew those sentiments in two years' time. Poor Cylrick has never spoken such things to Kyra. It definitely changes your perspective to hear them."

David seemed flustered for a bit. "I promise to write often."

Kyra nodded and wiped her tears. "I do as well. There is so much more I wish to know of you."

"And I you."

Just then, there was a slight rap upon the door. When the king answered it, a servant let them know their carriage was ready and waiting.

Kyra's mother looked up. "Did you order the carriage already?"

Henry nodded. "I felt it best. She needs rest in her own home. These beds are not the same."

They most certainly were not. Even the makeshift one her parents put together was not anything like what she was used to.

"Well, I had no idea!" Her mother seemed put out. "I wish you had consulted me first, dear. I could have used a night of sleep at least before we traveled back."

Again, David and her father exchanged a look as if they were privy to information Kyra and her mother were not. "What is it?" she asked.

"Nothing," Henry answered. "I feel it is best to remove you from this home as soon as possible. You risk infection every hour we wait, and I would like our physician to double-check all that the good doctor has advised. And we can only do that if we are home."

That made more sense. "Very well. Let us make haste. Perhaps he will not believe my legs cannot heal. Maybe I will be able to keep them." She then turned to David. "You have given me more hope than you know. I am anxious to begin this correspondence so I may truly get to know you better. You amaze me, and that is a very good thing indeed."

He grinned. "You have two years to recover, and then I am bringing you out into the pea fields again."

"What?" She laughed. "You would not dare."

"In your wheeled chair? Why not? Besides, I will be anxious to play our game again. This time, you will hold the basket and tell me how exceptionally handsome I look while I toss weeds in it."

"Ha. No doubt I will be pitching the whole basket of weeds upon your head!"

CHAPTER TWENTY-FIVE:

Six fairly miserable weeks later, Kyra was sitting up in her beautiful purple bed and lamenting her life. Their doctor had insisted he could save her legs, and that he had to attach long wooden rods down the sides of each limb and bandage them up tightly once the open wounds had healed. But he had to straighten her legs first, and that was the most excruciating pain she had ever experienced. Everyone was happy to see her in so much pain because it meant she could feel—yet honestly, she wished herself fully crippled and amputated a thousand times over than to feel her legs being forced back into place.

She felt trapped by large, mummified limbs without any relief. She could not wiggle, or scratch, or move an inch. There were days when she wondered if she was actually going mad. How she missed running and dancing and leaping, or really, just standing and walking.

Kyra sighed and stared glumly out her window, viewing the world outside moving without her. It was a horrid existence some days. Like today. And then other days, she could convince herself that all was not as bad as it seemed. Those were usually the days when her father or little brother or her lady's maid would play games with her. She was diverted enough not to become too sad.

And then there were days when she would be carried by the servants out to the garden and feel the fresh air and be reminded once more that the world was good, though her favorite days were the ones when David would write. He did not write nearly as often as she wished he would, but he was steady, and his correspondence was well written and informative and humorous, the type of thing she wished most in letters.

He had been busy gathering clues with his men and her father, and was in the process of capturing one of the bandits with hopes of the other close by. They had found out where the men lived—though David forgot to mention where. Even though she asked him in the last letter she sent, he forgot to include it when he responded.

Kyra was curious to see which kingdom seemed the most determined to see her fall. She was very grateful to see David so close to capturing the monsters. After she rang for a writing board and quill and ink, she sat up a little higher in her bed and began to answer the missive she had received from him the day before.

Dearest Prince David,

What a wonderful letter to receive. You lifted my spirits right away. I am so grateful you have nearly captured our bandits. I can imagine how pleased you must feel, and my father as well. We miss him dearly, but Mother knows he is where he is needed at present. Have you heard if the men have attacked anyone else? I surely hope they have not, and I am grateful for any tidbit of information you can give me. Heaven knows, such excitement helps me forget a little of the mediocre days that go by.

As for me, there are good days and then there are not-so-good days, but all in all, it is not the worst of life, I suppose. Thank you for inquiring. My rods are still in place, so my legs stick straight out, making me look extremely silly. The doctor has said I must keep them on for four more weeks. Four! He is hoping that by then, the breaks will have healed. But honestly, I could harm someone with these legs sticking straight out as they are. My poor mother must go all the way to my side to hug me. And when I am carried anywhere, it is the hardest thing for the staff to see that I do not knock anything over as I go. Uncle Herbert's painting, which was hung right outside my door, only lasted two days once the rods were in place. I managed to kick it clean off the wall and shatter the frame.

I am fortunate enough to have a dear family who wishes to entertain me with games and riddles and the like. And only just yesterday, my mother instructed that I be carried down the stairs and be set in the middle of the flower garden. How I enjoyed that. The butterflies were out, which was a little late for the end of summer, but there they were nonetheless. I am particularly grateful for the sunshine and good weather we are having up here.

What is the weather like for you? Is it warm, or has your autumn finally come? Or are you still battling the rain? And while we are on the subject, I have to ask, what is your favorite time of the year? I prefer now, the end of summer, just before fall begins—harvest time—right when the whole world begins to prepare for winter, yet it is still warm enough to take strolls in the dark and dream *of the excitement of the holidays to come. The lakes are at their warmest, the fish are biting in the lazy streams, and corn on the cob melts in your mouth.*

And before I close this, I have two more questions for you. One, what kingdom are you in? If it is mine, you and my father would surely not hide that from me, would you? I have asked you before, and you forgot to answer. Now I am even more curious than ever. So please do not forget this time.

For my second question, what is your favorite holiday? And more importantly, how do you like to spend that holiday? On your own, with family and friends? What do you do? When you get a moment, describe it for me so I understand.

I will be anxiously awaiting your next letter.

Sincerely,

Princess Kyra

CHAPTER TWENTY-SIX:

It had been a long rough couple of nights in the cold. David and his men had been given the perfect tip from the caretaker of a pub of where the last villain was known to live. They had easily captured the first. That filthy man was at the moment sitting in the dungeon of David's castle, awaiting the news from David's parents of what would happen to him. The second man still had not returned home, and David, King Henry, and several guards had been hiding out behind the foliage and trees near his cottage, waiting to pounce the moment he returned.

It had been their best tip yet, which had been confirmed when King Henry located his daughter's necklace inside the home. It had first belonged to the king's mother, and held the family crest stamped upon the back. There was no mistaking that this was the home of the man who had taken it from his daughter.

If only the blasted man would show up. Months ago, David would have left his guards to camp out and then return with the bandit. But that was before he met his brave Princess Kyra. Now, he had every desire to see this through to the end with his men and be there to help capture the wastrel. They were not without all the comforts of home, however. David had guaranteed that two of his men went back to the castle and returned with supplies daily during their journey.

When he received Kyra's letter, he was grateful to have some sort of distraction from the mundane waiting. He took it from the guard and then walked farther away from the small site and eagerly opened it. After reading the missive a few times, he leaned against a trunk and then pulled out his traveling case of quill, ink, and paper from the leather pouch within his overcoat pocket.

He had been hoping she would not notice that he skirted around the answer of where the bandit had been caught and where he currently was. There had been no reason to add more anxiety to her fragile state. However, he could not deny her the request. He nibbled on his lip a bit, pondering how best to share the news with her, finally deciding that frankly and openly would most likely be the best choice. There had already been too many secrets between them to begin with. If they were ever to achieve a normal relationship, they needed to trust each other with the facts.

David took a deep breath and began to write, using the edge of his leather pouch to support his paper.

Dear Princess Kyra,

Forgive me for not mentioning earlier where I am. It is with deep regret I need to inform you that we are in the kingdom of your betrothed, Prince Cylrick. Once we catch this second bandit—the first is awaiting trial at my castle—your father is convinced we will learn that your betrothed and his family were behind the whole scheme.

We have been past his castle more than once. Though we have not gone in to speak to the young prince, it is obvious that his castle is in sad disrepair. It looks like the kingdom has not had much money for some time. Deep in the midst of the pubs and local gambling clubs, there have been many people willing to talk. As far as we can tell after gathering bits and pieces, we have come up with the following story:

Several years before you were born, your grandfather and Prince Cylrick's grandfather had a very heated feud over a racing horse. No one is quite certain who was at fault, but as Prince Cylrick's grandmother lay on her deathbed, she begged her son to end the feud her late husband had created. After some thinking, your betrothal was arranged, but with some hidden animosity toward your family. Many people believe Prince Cylrick had become obsessed with an imagined debt your grandfather owed his. With his own kingdom in ruins from his grandfather's gambling habits, he was livid and desperate to attach himself to your wealth, and therefore has spent hours going mad, thinking of ways to strip you and your family of all their riches after you wed him.

We do not understand the correlation between the need to abduct you first instead of merely playing nice and wedding you, but each day, we uncover more of this absurd history. I will continue to hold out my full judgment until I know for certain that he was truly a part of this all.

Meanwhile, I am so grateful to hear the news of your legs. Though I am sorry they are painful, I, like the others around you, am very excited to hear you are feeling pain. It is a good sign. And although I expressed such gratitude to your doctor the last time I wrote, I feel the need to do so again. I am extremely happy he has not amputated your limbs as of yet. Each day you are whole makes me believe in miracles again. Let me reiterate how much it truly does not matter to me one whit if you have your legs or not, yet I feel it will boost your spirits if you did not have to lose them. Either way, my heart is still yours.

These weeks of chasing down the men who did this to you has allowed me much time to ponder life and how truly lacking I was of understanding the world around me. I have grown to respect your father daily for his insight and natural good sense, both in helping to capture the men and in finding them. I have also grown respectful of his need to insist we take two years to continue to grow and understand one another better. What I am finding is that not only am I enjoying our correspondence immensely and learning of you, but I am also learning much about me. Much that I did not know and am grateful to learn.

Your father is a very wise man, and his counsel is just. No matter how hard this becomes for each of us, I feel we will be stronger for doing what he has asked. I needed to understand myself more than I did. I needed to step up and learn what it meant to truly act as a ruler ought, not merely lying about, expecting others to do my bidding.

Now to stop all this seriousness for a moment and answer your questions.

My favorite weather... this is a very difficult question, actually. I find I do not really have a favorite. Instead, I enjoy change. I love each season as it is and would grow bored if things were always the same. When I am indoors and safely sheltered, I love the sound of rain upon the roof and the deep, roaring thunderstorms. I also love the promise of snow, the falling leaves, the warmth of a sunny day, and especially the windy, blustery days. In actuality, I love all types of weather. I feel as though each one brings a new promise and adventure with it. However, your late-summer scene does sound divine.

My favorite holiday would be my kingdom's Pea Harvest Festival in the middle of July. There are fantastic games, races, and carnivals, as well as many pea recipe contests, pea-eating contests, and archery contests— where the marksmen must hit the pea target. We have folk dancing, signing, theatrical performances, and prizes. Several, several prizes. There is such a fun sense of community during this time with all the preparation before and then cleanup after, as well as at the end, when the whole kingdom gives gifts to their families to celebrate the hope of a great harvest the next year. I have always loved this holiday and always will. There are so many memories of fun that surround that week. I cannot wait to share it with you.

Now you have brought to mind a couple of questions I must ask you. Do you like eating peas? And what are your thoughts on traveling and seeing the world?

Please take care, my dear. Hang in there, and keep your spirits up. Already, seven weeks have passed. Nearly two months. Let us continue to have our own adventures and make the most of this time. My heart is yours now and forever.

Love,
Prince David

CHAPTER TWENTY-SEVEN:

For four months, at least twice—sometimes three or four times—a week, Kyra faithfully wrote Prince David. She learned so very much about him. How he loved adorable forest creatures and hoped one day to have a small rescue home for the ones that had been abandoned by their parents or orphaned. She had never heard of such kindness to animals, and she could clearly see how he would be laughed at for even suggesting the idea to anyone else. Yet he was so very passionate about it, she did not have the heart to say something negative in response. Who was she to crush his dreams? Besides, would he not help several animals in the process?

Such revelations from David allowed her to open up and share her fear of heights and of things falling upon her.

When she had awoken from her fitful sleep, Kyra yawned through a dreadful headache. She blinked her eyes and then blinked again when she stared at the white note sitting upon a silver plate near her bed. She grinned happily, leaned over, and snatched it up. Her hands shook as she began to read, feeling very much as if she were not worthy of such an amazing, adventurous man.

It was fascinating to read of your fears as you so generously shared with me. Put into such detail, I can quite easily imagine them being something that would scare me as well. Though, after pondering your question for a good several hours last night and then again this morning, there is only one fear that frightens me and holds my heart in such gripping anxiety as you have explained. Would you like to know what it is?

Of course you do. It is what you have asked for... Yet, you must understand that even writing this now, I am shaking. My handwriting is becoming horridly messy, my breathing shallow, and a fine sheen of sweat has popped out all over my brow and upper lip. Dearest Princess Kyra, my greatest fear in the world is losing you. I cannot bear the thought. Every day is yours, every word, every deed I do, I carry you with me—would she like what I have just done? Would she like the taste of the scone I have eaten? Would she have liked the person I have spoken to? Or the dress that young woman was wearing? Each day, I fantasize what your reactions would be as if you were here beside me.

I could not, simply would not fathom you gone. I fear I have grown even fonder of your gumption, your joys, your strengths, your ideals, and your sorrows than you could ever imagine. So please keep your soul open to receiving this fearful prince.

Having spent a good portion of the night convincing herself that she was unfit and unable to create any sort of love within the heart of such a prince as David, the letter had caused her chest to swell in warmth and with new affirmation. How much she needed to hear that his worst fear was her leaving! How much such words from him reminded her not to give up.

Kyra slipped from the bed and had her maid help her put the steel harness about her waist and then attach each leg to long rods that went down the length of her sides. Those long rods were connected to a front portion she could push against. It also had long rods that reached the floor that had wheels on them. With the help of the makeshift steel contraption, she stood up and pushed against the thing, painfully dragging her legs behind, forcing them to take the impossible steps that would one day allow her to surprise her love with her ability to walk.

But it took time. And pain. So very much pain. And perspiration and several thousands of tears—working through true grit and determination to accomplish the impossible.

The day he had written to say both men who had harmed her were shipped off from these lands, she had decided to surprise him. He had done so very much for her that when the two years were over, it would be the greatest of joys to see his face once he saw her walking toward him. Then he would know that while he tirelessly worked for her, so had she for him.

After weeping for some time, Kyra then picked up his letter and finished it, this time reading the last page that contained the most important information their correspondence had produced for months.

Kyra, I write the last portion of this letter with news I can hardly express, so bear with me as I attempt to reveal all that has come to light. Your father will be coming home soon—he may even beat this missive to your kingdom, and he will clarify any questions you may have, and hopefully affirm the truthfulness of all we learned yesterday.

Prince Cylrick was, as we feared, deeply involved in your kidnapping and the accident with your coach. After following several leads through family members of the servants who work in his castle, we were able to ascertain that he had collected your missing servants, and they were even then within his castle holding cells and being treated as prisoners. Yesterday evening, we staged a siege on the castle and rescued those still living. Your coachman and two outriders managed to survive the cruel torture techniques used to extract any information about your family your intended could get. I am deeply sorry to report, two others did not survive, and your father will bring those names home to you.

His motives are unclear, though several of the servants' family members all speak of reports of the drunken jealous rages the prince would fly into as he thought of your family's money. Instead of merely waiting for you to come, wooing you as he ought, he had spent years before then growing bitter in jealousy to the point that many believe he went mad.

Which is perhaps the hardest of this to write because his actions do not make sense, nor may they ever. We have him detained within our castle walls and are unsure what to do with him. He is a great harm to the other kingdoms while in this state. Your father has suggested that we hold an emergency meeting within a week or so, calling all kings to come forth and vote together on what should be done with the reprobate.

After mulling it over, I have come to the conclusion that he was still hoping to wed you—but first wanted to panic you by hiring kidnappers to frighten and remind you that you are not as special as you believe yourself. That because you have money, you deserved to experience pain of some sort before you wed him. Though, it backfired when his men were not able to get you at first.

Your servants ran straight to him to implore for his help in recovering you, which your coachman revealed he agreed to do. Then Cylrick promptly had them all sent to the cellars. There his greatest madness began to show as he questioned them all about you and your family in such cruel ways.

I fear I must leave you with this disturbing news. I am needed elsewhere at the moment, but I will answer all that I can when respond again.

Know that you are loved. I am so grateful you are safe and did not marry him.

Love,
David

Kyra dropped the letter once more, this time in shock, and then rang for her mother. To think—had Prince Cylrick been kind and wooed her as he ought to have, she would be married to the monster now. Her hands shook as her mother came in the room. Without a word, Kyra passed the letter over, and then about half an hour later was greeted by her father, who came up to her room directly after arriving home. He might have smelled of adventure, firewood, and horse, but he was finally home.

The small family embraced and wept and then embraced again.

* * *

Precisely two years and two weeks from the date Kyra's father declared they had to wait, Princess Kyra married her dashing, daring Prince David. It was a glorious ceremony with hundreds of beautiful white flowers strung together in long strands to decorate her kingdom's beautiful chapel.

The couple had long before planned in detail, through countless letters, their life together. David had already began to build a beautiful castle of their own on some land granted him by his father. Meanwhile, they were to live with King Henry and Queen Patricia until the home was complete.

Kyra kept to her word and managed, with the aid of her steel contraption, to miraculously surprise both her father and David by walking very slowly up the aisle.

Five years later, with the aid of a cane and two little ones surrounding her, Kyra stepped over the threshold of her new home. David wanted very much to carry her into the castle, but she was determined to walk on her own two legs.

Life was peaceful and happy for the couple. Even though there were years of trials that somehow found their way into laughter, they continued to thrive. Those two little children grew up to have nine delightful grandchildren between them. Kyra and David together learned the meaning of love, growth, and most especially, the value of finding joy through strife—and peas. Their own crops were some of the greatest in the land, and some said, even better than the king and queen's—though David and Kyra would never admit to such a thing. At least out loud.

THE END

Jenni James is the busy mother of ten kids and has over thirty published book babies. She's an award-winning, bestselling author who works full time from home and dreams about magical things and then writes about what she dreams. Some of her works include the Jane Austen Diaries (*Pride & Popularity, Emmalee, Persuaded...*), the Jenni James Faerie Tale Collection (*Cinderella, Snow White, Rumplestiltskin, Beauty and the Beast...*), the Andy & Annie series for children, *Revitalizing Jane: Drowning, My Paranormal Life, Not Cinderella's Type,* and the Austen in Love series. When she isn't writing up a storm, she's chasing her kids around their new cottage and farm in Fountain Green, entertaining friends at home, or kissing her amazingly hunky hubby. Her life is full of laughter, crazy, and sunshine.

You can follow her on.

Facebook: authorjennijames

Twitter: Jenni_James

Instagram author Jenni James

Amazon Page (follow to get updates when a new book is released):

 Amazon.com/jennijames

She loves to hear from her readers. You can contact her via—

Email: thejennijames@gmail.com

www.thejennijames.com

Snail Mail:

Jenni James

PO Box 449

Fountain Green, UT 84632

Other books by Jenni James:

The Jane Austen Diaries

Pride & Popularity

Persuaded

Emmalee

Mansfield Ranch

Northanger Alibi

Sensible & Sensational

Regency Romance

The Bluestocking and the Dastardly, Intolerable
Scoundrel

Lord Romney's Exquisite Widow

Lord Atten Meets His Match (2017)

Cinderella and the Phantom Prince

Austen in Love

My Pride, His Prejudice

Jane & Bingley

My Persuasion

Modern Fairy Tales

Not Cinderella's Type

Sleeping Beauty: Back to Reality

Beauty IS the Beast

Children's Book:

Andy & Annie: A Ghost Story

Andy & Annie: Greeny Meany

Prince Tennyson

Women's Fiction

Revitalizing Jane: Drowning

Revitalizing Jane: Swimming (2017)

Revitalizing Jane: Crawling (2017)

Chapter 1

"Indy! Come on—let's go."

I groaned as I rolled over on the grass. This so wasn't my life. Why did PE have to be so hard, anyway? Was the coach's goal to kill everyone who was seriously PE challenged? I needed an excuse card or something. Like one of those "get out of jail free" cards. In fourth grade, my friend Gabby Mineyard had one from her doctor because of some fictitious disease. Okay, so it probably wasn't fictitious, but I swear she was completely normal and could do anything at all during the summer—anything. Like ride a bike, go swimming, climb trees—anything. Until school started. Then there was that glorious "exempt from PE" card again.

"Indy!"

Maxton was still yelling at me. Couldn't he see I was in pain? As in, suffering here? Whatever—it didn't matter. Ms. Bullington was going to come back around the Flagstaff High School track with the other runners any minute and chew me out anyway. Time to suck it up.

I groaned again for good measure and rolled over onto my knees. I took the hand offered me and got up. I was about to thank Maxton for being there, but to my knowledge, Maxton's chest wasn't quite so large, and he wasn't so tall, either. I jerked my head up and came face-to-face with the hottest junior in school, Bryant Bailey.

"What?" I asked, not willing to give him an inch this time. "Why are you here?"

A playful grin spread across his face. "Why are you so mean to me?"

I glared over his shoulder at Maxton for not telling me Bryant was there. He just shrugged back.

Then I turned my glare to Bryant. "You need to come with a warning label or something so people can be prepared when you show up." I pushed past him and grabbed my water bottle. It didn't matter if Ms. Bullington was angry at me or not, there was no way I was sticking around PE another minute. Lamely—literally—I began to limp off the grass, across the track field, and toward the building behind the bleachers. Dang my stupid foot, anyway. I was always twisting my ankle when I tried to run. Always.

Some people were born with grace, and others were meant to watch graceful people from far away. Like miles away. It wasn't hard to guess which category of people I fit into.

Bryant followed me. *Of course.* "Are you really going to blow me off?"

I tried to whirl around, but I forgot about my foot. However, my foot didn't forget it was twisted, and it reminded me—sharply. "Yeesh!" I headed straight. Apparently, walking forward was better than turning around. "Do you expect anything else, Bryant? Seriously? I could so kill you right now, and you know it. In fact, I'm pretty sure that in seventeen states, it'd be legal to kill you. Most people would call it self-defense."

He rolled his eyes, but matched his super-long stride to my shorter one. "You can run away all you want. I'm still going to make it up to you one day."

"No, you're not. I don't want you to. The best way to make anything up is just to leave me alone. Please."

"Do you really despise me that much?"

"Yes."

"Liar."

Urgh. What was I going to have to do to get this guy off my back? I stopped. "If you want to make it up to me, go away. I'm fine. I need some time alone to process it, not to be reminded every five seconds."

"But I've apologized a hundred times. I had no idea it was there. I didn't see it. It was an accident. And every time I see you, I feel awful. I don't even know what to do. I'm not some weird, awful guy—you've gotta give me a chance and let me make it up to you!"

All at once, my heart was heavy and my foot hurt and my chest felt like the Hulk was squeezing it and I wanted out of this dang school. Away from Bryant Bailey and everyone else who had ruined everything special in my life. I just wanted not to remember terrible things. Was that so hard? Except, every time I turned around, there was Bryant again—caught up in his own psycho-codependency or something where he wanted everyone to like him and everything to be fine. But you know what? I wasn't going to like him. Not now, not ever. And it was never going to get better.

So he needed to deal with it somewhere else. What's done was done, and that's that. Showing up all the time, trying to make me feel happy or something was certainly not going to fix anything.

I opened the outside door to the gym and limped inside.

"Cindy, please…"

This time, I did whirl around just as he came into the building. Ouch. "Cindy?" How did he know my real name? My mom's name. No one knew that name. Not even Maxton, and he knew me back when my mom was still alive.

Bryant must've taken my facing him as a good sign because in the next second, he was holding my arm and looking at me seriously. "Will you forgive me?"

Didn't he hear a word I just said? I lost it. In retrospect, I probably shouldn't have, but I was done. Yeah, I was a little mean, but this guy was getting borderline stalkerish, and enough was enough. As in, I was completely and totally through with being reminded of everything that'd gone wrong in my life. And calling me Cindy was the last straw.

I tugged my arm away. "No, Bryant. I won't forgive you for killing my cat! That cat was from my mom. The last gift I'd gotten from her before she died in a car accident. It just so happens that I was named after my mom, and until now, she was the only person who ever called me Cindy."

His eyes widened in shock, and his mouth opened slightly. Thankfully, he didn't speak, or I might've punched him.

"Now, if you will kindly leave me alone to mourn the loss of the last gift I was ever given, who was one of my best friends—and no! I don't expect you to know anything about how awesome cats are, okay?—but she was, and now she's gone. Because you had to speed around by my street and—"

He pulled me in for a big hug. "I'm sorry, Indy. I'm so, so sorry."

"And then to top it all off, you come out with Cindy? Why? *How?*" I tried to push away, but his arms were wrapped around me too tightly. "You know what—I don't want to know. All I care about is when this pain will stop. When will I be able to think about happy things again and just be normal?"

He said it before I could. "Never. You'll never be the same again."

"No." I sniffed. And that's when I realized why he was hugging me so tight. "Dang it. I'm crying?" I pulled away this time, and he let me go. Yep, the whole front of his shirt was wet.

Bryant Bailey made me cry. My sophomore year of high school. I hadn't cried since my mom died. Not when I had to move into my aunt and uncle's house and live in their creepy basement room, not when my cousins made fun of me and told me how ugly I was. And I didn't cry when I became their stupid servant, when my aunt left me with all the chores since my cousins were too involved in after-school activities to have time to clean. And I didn't even cry when Mrs. Wiggins, my cat died—I was too angry to cry. Yet, now here I was, standing in the school gym and crying in front of the one guy I detested most.

And then I said it—the most immature words that have ever left my mouth. "I hate you." I cringed as soon as I said them, but they were out and they were the truth, so I looked up at him . . . and saw Bryant for possibly the first time in my life. Really saw him.

His dark eyes searched mine, long and hard, as if they were prying out every single one of my secrets. This tall, extremely good-looking dark-haired prince-type guy just stared at me. He should've been chasing the pretty girls at school, or working out in the weight room, or writing some amazing symphony that would make him incredibly famous, but instead, he was standing there with me. Then those worried brows of his came together and his mouth turned down a little and he spoke the words that honestly broke me. I have no idea why—but later in my creepy basement room all alone, I sobbed and sobbed and sobbed. For the first time in years, I let everything out.

"I hate me too," he whispered.

And then he kissed me on the cheek, whispered "Sorry" in my ear, and then left.

A sneak peak of The Bluestocking and the Dastardly, Intolerable Scoundrel:

CHAPTER ONE:

Lady Lacey Lamb, Viscountess Melbourne, was in high fidgets as she paced indignantly across the intricately woven rug in the library of her newly purchased townhome on Green Street. "Are you certain it was my name the insufferable swines were bandying about?"

She swirled around to face her second gardener, a respectable Mr. Toppens, who had only this moment returned from the errand she had sent him on earlier that morning. The old garden was in shambles, and one could not think when one's garden was in shambles, which is why it was imperative she bring up all of the gardening staff to the new home immediately. Toppens had been to fetch the seedlings she arranged to be picked up and had come back not only with the seedlings, but also with the most hideous piece of shameful gossip that had crossed this threshold yet.

"Yes, my lady. I came directly home soon as I heard." He fidgeted with his hat and stepped from one foot to the other.

"Thunderation!" she grumbled as she spun on her heel again, her brown muslin gown spinning with her. "Abominable. Unspeakable toads."

"Now, calm down," Pantersby, her normally sympathetic butler, attempted to soothe her. "You do not know the whole of it yet. It could be mere gabblemongers having a laugh at your expense."

"My expense! That is what causes me the most ire. No matter how anyone chooses to look at this, it has been done at my expense."

Both men jumped as she flung the small book she had been clutching upon the chiseled table before her.

This would not do. She was not some horrific shrew of a woman who shouted the place down. Placing her hand to her throat, she took a deep breath to calm the roaring of anger in her ears and struggled to ask coolly, her voice shaking a bit unevenly, "Tell me again, Toppens. What precisely did occur outside of White's?"

Toppens glanced anxiously at Pantersby and cleared his throat. "Lord Alistair Compton was in the midst of the throng."

"Are you confident it was him?"

"Yes, my lady. It was his height, standing a good head and shoulders above the rest—could not have been anyone else but he."

She nodded and closed her eyes. "Continue."

"He and a right large group of nobs came out of White's all boisterous and lively like, the whole lot of them laughing up a storm—never heard so much racket in my life. So, as I was waiting for the line of coaches to ease up a bit—seems as though everyone is coming to town today—I looked over and saw them all. And they were loud as crows, they were, shouting to the skies how as their betting at White's would give Lord Compton ten-to-one odds to get you, Lady Icey Lamb, Viscountess Melbourne, to fall dreadfully in love him by the end of the Season."

Apprehension gripped her chest as Lacey took another deep breath. This could not be happening. This simply could not be. "Icey? They think I am made of ice? Merely since I refuse to become a flirtatious chit in their presence? Now, because I declined to stand up with that buffoon Compton at Lady Huffington's ball, they must place wagers as if I were some token to be won? Infuriating villains. How dare they?" Lacey would have found another book to throw, but stopped herself. There was no need to ruin a perfectly magnificent library because of a bunch of nodcocks.

"'Tis why I came straight to you, my lady. I supposed you must know immediately to put this to stops."

"Yes." Her eyes lit up on the older silver-haired man. "Pantersby, is there anything that can be done?"

"Apart from castrating the lot of them?"

Lacey gasped and threw her hand to her mouth to stop the surprised giggle that was attempting this very moment to show itself. "Pantersby! Why, I never!"

He stood prim and proper, his uniform sharp, though one mischievous side of his mouth turned up the merest bit. "Yes, my lady?"

She gave in and a smile broke out, then a chuckle. Pantersby always had a way of helping her find the lighter side of any situation. But this was a larger mess than she had ever been in. Nonplussed, she sat down upon the nearest chair, her brown skirts in a wild array, as she took in the gravity of the situation. "Why can I not have peace?" She sighed. "This is precisely why I cannot abide *le beau monde* or the Season. I loathe coming here. A bunch of false gossipy twits trying to outdo each other in the most repulsive display of the marriage mart. Little gels with their hopeful mamas, wistful to catch the lucky looks of a mere stranger." She let out a very unladylike groan. "It is the most pitiful excuse of an existence there is—and I must endure it year after year."

"Well, if I may be so bold?"

She waved her hand. "Go ahead, Pantersby. You are most welcome to say whatsoever comes to mind, for nothing can be as dreadful as this. And Toppens, you may go. I thank you for the information. Though shocking, I am more grateful to have it than not."

Once the second gardener left, Pantersby continued, "You have two options here." He took a step forward. "You can pack up and run to the country again, as you are usually wont to do—this will force Lord Compton to forfeit his outrageous bet."

"Or?"

"You gird up your armor and stay to commence a battle."

Intrigued, Lacey sat up. "How so?"

"You teach that youth a thing or two about manners, for one. A bluestocking does not become a prestigious bluestocking because she is a simpleton. No, my lady, you have an opportunity to school the brat and set him down a peg or two."

One slim finger thoughtfully tapped her mouth. "I do have the upper hand, thanks to Toppens."

"That you do."

She scrunched her brow. "But I despise petty games like this."

"You can learn to enjoy them, you know."

"I can?" She stood up. There was no reason she should be in sulks over this. "So I can. And I will." She walked over to Pantersby and nodded once before stepping past him into the gallery. "I shall teach this dastardly, intolerable scoundrel the foolishness of placing one's bet before his comrades." A small grin began to form itself upon her features once more as an indignant brow arched. "Society may come and go as they please and attend their silly soirees and galas. I am here for Parliament alone. Women cannot yet attend, but the newspapers are quick in London, and my brother, Lord Melbourne, will continue to tell me the Whig ondits. I will have all the fascinating knowledge I need to entertain myself. However, this need not mean that I should be put out between sessions."

She walked to the center of the vestibule, placed her simple, unadorned bonnet atop her fiery red hair, and tied the bow rakishly to the side. Then she allowed Pantersby to slide her green woolen pelisse about her shoulders. "Please have Jameson bring the curricle around."

"Are you to go out alone, my lady?"

Lacey sighed as she tugged on her kid-leather gloves. "Do you think I ought not?"

"You know very well what I think. 'Tis too dangerous for you to be out and about without Mrs. Crabtree, or a footman at the least."

"If *men* can banter my name willy-nilly all over the place, I see no reason why it is not permissible to grant me the opportunity to defend myself and do the equivalent."

"You are not going to White's! 'Tis a gentleman's club. Please say that you are not."

Lacey closed her eyes and took yet another deep breath. Life was not just, and Pantersby was fortunate that she esteemed him as family or that outburst would have harmed him greatly.

"Begging your pardon, ma'am. I do not know what came over me."

She took her reticule from the same side table where all the rest of the folderols had been and then met his eyes.

"Do not worry. You are only attempting to make me see reason. To remind me of these confounded rules of town. No, I had not one notion to attend White's and place my own wager, making a fool and mockery of Lord Compton. Why should I ever do that?" Lacey tugged forcefully on her pelisse and gestured for Pantersby to open the door for her.

"No, I will allow my brother to avenge my wrongs. And as surely as I speak the truth of the matter to him, he will most certainly place the bet for me, and then Lord Compton and I will be on even ground, no?"

Pantersby gave a smug grin. "No, Lady Lamb. Not one whit of you shall be on even ground with such a man. Indeed, you are, and always will be, scores above him."

"Thank you, Pantersby."

He opened the door to the drudgery of London's finest attempts at weather and sent a footman scurrying to the lady's side to await the curricle.

"And what of the wager? Have you thought of a sufficient reply to his?"

Lacey smiled at the bottom of the steps of her new townhome and said, "Why, it will be to guarantee that he shall tumble topsy-turvy and head over heels in love with the Icey Lady Lamb." She chuckled at Pantersby's face above her. "The best part is, Pantersby, I have enough to my name that I can easily lose the despicable wager. Lord Compton, I believe, is such a wastrel of man, he does not. Either way, he fails, and perhaps next Season, he will learn to be a bit less of a libertine and more of a gentleman. Why, his mama may thank me when this is all through."